Battle Horse of Kings

Battle Horse of Kings

Norma Grimes

Published by Norma Grimes.
Apartado 1078
Sucursal 1
Estepona 29680
Malaga
Spain

BATTLE HORSE OF KINGS

IBSN 978-84-697-6649-1

Book formatted by www.bookformatting.co.uk.

Contents

Acknowledgements

Geoff, Samantha, Shelly and Kit, Elke Schulze, Francisco Tineo Vasquez, Christopher Rushton and Vetequin Estepona.

Literature

The Spanish Horse ... Fernando d'Andrade
Xenophon ... works of

Ganador V Spanish State Stallion

There can only be one fitting tribute for Ganador, my noble Spanish stallion. It is this trilogy of books about his life and history ... the words of which will enable others to share his extraordinary magic. I hope those who read my account of Ganador's life will remember his bravery and magic forever...

I miss you my noble white stallion... Oh, how I miss you...

Norma Grimes (author)

Also by Norma Grimes

Battle Horse Trilogy

The Story of Ganador (book one)

Son of the Wind (book two)

Battle Horse of King's (book three)

About The Author

Norma is a professional musician and freelance writer on classical equitation. She lives in Andalucia with husband Geoff and daughter Samantha, where she keeps the love of her life Iberian Horses. She studied classical riding in Portugal and Vienna, is an associate of the Royal College and Licentiate of the Royal Academy and has taught in colleges within the UK.

To Samantha

Al Andaluz

'On its brow it carries the brilliant mark of the morning

The stars fall back when it starts to move

And the clouds cannot catch it no matter how fast they fly

Ask the wind how fast this horse can run

For none can tell but the wind alone…'

Iberian Horseman

Prologue.

Last night in my dreams I returned to the freezing cold day in March, when I saw the advert that changed my life. Tearing the wrapping from around my favorite must read magazine I watched it fall open, somewhere in the middle, and there, right before my eyes were the words I had waited to see ... for seven long years:

'Ganador V, Spanish State Registered Stallion, Baroque lineage, reasonable...'

For a time it felt like the earth had stopped spinning, so I read the words three more times just to make sure they were there. When I told Sue my groom, she answered in her annoying palm reader's voice.

"Sounds a bit dodgy," she said with a knowing expression written all over her face. "What's the catch?"

And then partner Geoff walked into the room and added his bit,

"Spanish stallions do not live in scrap yards and neither are they reasonable," he said drily "And driving six hundred miles in a horsebox is a long way to go to find out."

"How do you know he lives in a scrap yard?" I asked wearily.

"Because I rang the number just now and the place is called 'Adams Scrap.' I need proof, could be a waste of time," said Geoff. And Sue nodded her head in agreement.

"But I know he's there," I replied. "My friend Antony tells me you find this breed in the strangest of places."

And with Geoff's words ringing in my ears we drove through the night from North Yorkshire to South East England.

When we arrived at our destination I felt shocked, there were no houses and no stables. Not even any fields. The address was that of

1

an industrial scrap yard with what looked to be a Gypsy encampment somewhere in the middle.

"You've brought me all this way to see skips and Gypsies..." said a freezing cold Geoff. But before he could say one more word a man with a limp emerged from behind an army of skips. He smiled and waved his cap.

"You folks must be from the high hills of Yorkshire, come down to see our Ganador." Following bowing, he shook hands and said, "Follow me." He led us through mountains of rubbish until suddenly we arrived in a clearing, or to be precise at the Gypsy camp. Here, he gestured to some steep, metal steps. "Come into my palace," he ordered, "the doors at the top." So we followed him up the steps and into his 'palace.' It was lovely and warm and shone of gold just about everywhere.

"Sit ye down and drink this warm tea," he said kindly. And sitting in front of the caravan stove we thawed out and ate breakfast served by the lady of the caravan, who everyone called 'Mother.'

After breakfast Adams led us to a muddy area someplace round the back of his wagon. He pointed to a ramshackle railway cabin, "Ganador's stable," he said ever so proudly.

"Finest creature to walk this earth he is."

Shafts of brilliant morning light shimmered through the open doorway casting glittering strips of silver across the stallion's neck. Ganador stood like a statue, chained to the back wall of the cabin. He never moved a muscle; he just stared into my eyes. Arrogance seemed to radiate from him and for a few minutes I felt in limbo land...my feet refused to move, my eyes seemed mesmerized by his. Right in front of me, amongst the squalor of human rubbish stood the most magnificent horse I had ever seen.

"Take your time Lass, drink his beauty in," said Adams. "There's no need to hurry."

I don't think I could have hurried, for I gazed at a horse through the mists of time, a wild fighting creature from another time, a forgotten time that began somewhere in mythology. I knew immediately that standing before me was a Spanish Stallion of the finest lines. What he was doing in a scrap yard could only be guessed at, and to be honest I no longer cared.

"He's thin," said Geoff from somewhere out of view. Geoff was correct; his once elegant body was on the verge of becoming angular. But I never noticed his leanness; I'd fallen in love with this Kingly horse, with an intensity I'd never known before.

"Gaze into his big black beautiful eyes," Adams ordered, "and you see a King." Adams held out his arm and stood a little closer to Ganador. The stallion's expression darkened menacingly … but all was too late. Ganador took aim, and bit his only un-bandaged finger hard. This was a planned move by the stallion, achieved in a fraction of a second. Wrapping a hanky around his bleeding finger, he took refuge behind Geoff. Ganador did not look afraid, if anything he looked defiant. Angrily he shook the chain, as if to warn him.

It was then he whinnied, his call was hauntingly beautiful, the notes clear and bell like. This mysterious creature was trying to communicate in his own heartrending way. "It's his song of the earth…" I whispered in awe.

Ganador listened carefully, his ears pointed and alert, his eyes fixed on the stable door. Striking the floor and shaking the chain he was tied with, Ganador awaited the coming of a friend.

"What a good Lad ye are Mark, coming to help tha dad," whined Adams as son Mark entered the stable.

Mark did not reply to his father, instead, he spoke to Ganador. "Where's me beauty, where's me Lad," he said softly as he scratched the stallion's nose. Ganador responded with soft musical cries… and Mark pressed his cheek against the stallion's awesome head. Ganador observed a lack of fear in Mark and I felt a bond of friendship between them.

"He's a brave oss my Ganador, to be sure, he's a fearless lad." Mark said proudly. "When the men are out Ganador patrols the yard. Anything strange and he's there, better than a guard dog this lad is."

"Is Ganador trained as a guard horse?" I stared at Mark in total disbelief. "But horses don't guard…"

"This lad does!" Mark laughed at my lack of knowledge.

"Ganador protects his territory like it's in his blood."

"Has he ever savaged anyone?" I whispered to Mark. Thank goodness Geoff's not listening.

"Thieves don't come complaining do they now?" Mark's laughter died away to a faint echo in the far distance.

And then my dream ended, it disappeared. I tried to waken up, but my mind felt locked, taken over by this other world we call dreams...

Suddenly I heard a voice; the sound was different to Mark's, nothing like any normal voice, it echoed as if from speakers in a vast auditorium.

"You have to pass a test before he's yours," the voice blared out.

I didn't argue, I had no alternative but to go along with whatever this voice ordered.

"What does the test comprise of?" I asked the mystery voice.

"You must journey through a vision where the past controls the future..."

And then I heard a knocking noise, it became louder and more persistent...

1 'Off to Seville'

5 a.m. North Yorkshire Moors, March 30 1981

I awoke to the sound of rain hammering against window panes and a west wind howling from the moors. Shivering, I grabbed two extra blankets, paused to look at the clock, and snuggled down into delicious warmth. I vaguely remember the phone ringing, but it might have been a dream, the sound was so far away...

"Those dogs have taken my slippers again," Geoff muttered irritably. "Why do you let them in the bedroom?" But I didn't reply, the world of sleep carried me back into my dreams.

When I awoke and looked at the clock it was five fifty. The time had passed in a flash. At that moment I recalled the phone ringing and Geoff's missing slipper. Where was he? As if to answer my question the bedroom door opened with a creak and he walked in carrying early morning tea.

"Are you awake?" He placed the cups down and sat on the bed.

"Who rang?"

"Mum rang earlier," he spoke hesitantly as if unsure of my response. "She needs you over there."

"What do you mean ... needs me over there? Mum's in Seville, not the next town."

"She sounds down, definitely not her usual self. It must be difficult being alone after all those years with Dad. So, I booked you a flight out which departs at four thirty... today."

"But I don't want to fly anywhere, what about shopping and the horses?"

"Listen love, mum wants to see 'you,' not fancy clothes. Shelly

5

can shop, and I'll see to the horses. Just take a weekend case and have a nice time. A week or two in Seville will do you a world of good." So I stopped arguing…what was the point?

After packing my smallest case, I walked down to the stables to say goodbye to Shelly and the horses. For a few moments I stood silently, enjoying Ganador's swift graceful movements. And then he whinnied; it was a vibrant stallion call that echoed over the valley. On hearing the disturbance Shelly put her head round the tack room door.

"Believe you're off to Seville," she said. "Some people have all the luck."

"Wish I was staying here…"

"You're worrying about the horses, I can tell. Well don't…" she said in a commanding voice. "Just go, and enjoy being warm…"

"Don't be too hard on Kit…" I pleaded. "He's good at straightening the muck heap if nothing else." Part time groom Kit had been downgraded to a farm laborer by Shelly, until he could think clearly…

"Promise to be kind," she said. "But I'm not letting him near the horses. He's not ready yet, and maybe he never will be."

Before I climbed into the land rover I took one last look at the hills of north Yorkshire. It was a dramatic scene, too lovely to be real, more like a painting. The heavy rain in the night had brought snow to the summits. Brush strokes of silver sparkled from the highest hills, mist clouds shrouded the valley. I loved the hills…

Slowly I drove away. I drove through the town of Todmorden and then westwards towards Manchester.

At four p.m. I fastened my seat belt and watched the runway disappear into rain cloud. As the big jet leveled off, a man in the next seat began to hum flamenco rhythms. The sound of his voice brought back memories of Pepe, the way he'd sung flamenco cante at the Romany wedding…a night I would never forget… and memories of the phone call that led me to his door, or more correctly, to his living wagon door came flooding back.

The day was the fourteenth of July when I received the call, less than eight months ago, but I remembered the day clearly, as it was marked on the calendar with the words, 'Ganador's four month anniversary, still can't believe he's mine!'

When the phone rang I shouted to Shelly, 'please answer it Shelly,' and I can still see her surprised look, as soon as she heard the voice.

"Norma..." she hissed across the room. "It's for you. A man from a scrap yard, name of Adams. I wonder if it's the Gypsy..."

As I walked over to the phone I suddenly felt nervous. "Wonder what he wants after all this time?" And Shelly pressed the receiver into my hand.

"Find out..." she said.

"It's Adams here, Adams from the scrap yard! Surely you remember the day you bought Ganador?"

"I'll never forget the day..."

"Mother and Mark wept the day Ganador left us, missed him so we have. But today, I'm ringing about a happy event! I'm inviting Norma, Geoff and Ganador to Mark's wedding. He's marrying a Spanish Lass, she's called Evita."

Now, I felt surprised, inviting a horse to a wedding didn't fit in with any marital plans that I knew of.

"Did you say Ganador?"

"He's number one on the guest list so he is. At a Romany wedding, a white holy horse is more important than the vows or the ring. A blessing from the God's it is. I'll make it worth Geoff's while. Everything has a price so it does..."

As Adams nattered on in his sing song voice, memories of the day I first saw Ganador flashed through my mind. There he stood a miracle of equine creation, in a scrap yard run by Gypsies. From the moment I saw him ... I had to have him. You see, I fell in love with this magnificent creature and I wanted him with a longing I'd never felt before.

But any similarities to the usual way of buying a horse ended right there. If and when a Gypsy sells a horse, it entails certain procedures which begin with a strange ritual called 'Romany horse trading'. Something Geoff and I were not on familiar terms with.

"If you want to buy Ganador," Adams explained patiently, "we traveling folks have a way of doing business. A gentleman's agreement so it is. So we all know where we stand!" And so we followed him into his caravan, with no idea what might happen next. "If we all stand round the table…" said Adams.

"Leave it to me," whispered Geoff. "And try to smile."

So I left everything with Geoff. At that moment Adams son Mark brought over a bottle of whisky and four glasses. After filling each glass to the rim, he gave Geoff a word of advice. "Start with a low bid," Mark hissed across the table. "And then we're off!"

So we stood round the table and waited for this bizarre Romany ritual to start. Mark placed us in position, 'I'll stand opposite Norma, and Geoff across from Dad,' said the young Gypsy. He winked as he encouraged Geoff to start the bidding, and said, 'Listen hard and remember not to laugh…'

"Eight pound bid," said Geoff. Adams slapped his hand then emptied his glass.

"Make it eight thousand and we might do business!" replied Adams. Now the hand slapping gained speed.

"Make it eight hundred and not a penny more," said Geoff. "Horses don't grow younger."

"The oss was bred by a King!!" shrieked Adams. Slowly, Geoff raised his bid, in the time honored way of traveling men. Not with a pen, nor a vet, but simply the slap of a hand … plus a tot of whisky. Geoff tried to negotiate his way through the perils of this strange method of buying a horse, but it was not his forte … he slapped at the wrong time and ended up paying over three hundred pounds more than his final bid. Something Geoff had never recovered from…'

"Are you still there?" Adams said. He was pleading now, probably wondering if I'd put the phone down. "There's a spare bedroom in the wagon, and a stable for Ganador…"

Two weeks later we drove down to South East England with Ganador, the most important guest at the Romany wedding, the white holy horse. When Mark led him through the scrap yard, then down the path to the old cabin, I felt a pang of guilt, for the place held memories I wanted to forget.

On the morning of the wedding I was taken to meet the bride's father Pepe, and his beautiful wife Mariapi.

When I first saw Pepe, he sat on the steps of a large luxurious living wagon, singing flamenco cante ... the most startlingly handsome man I'd ever set eyes upon. He thanked me for bringing Ganador to his daughter's wedding ... 'for making Evita happy.' He told me that Ganador was Evita's favorite stallion and how she cried for days when he was sold to England.

"So you know Ganador?" For some reason I felt shocked.

"I manage the Yeguada where he was bred...," he replied.

Pepe placed a card in my hand. "When you come to Seville I'll tell you his story..." He bowed low, hand over heart and touched my hand, as if to remind me that 'he' held the key. I felt his energy, his emotions.

"But how will I contact you?"

"I have a flamenco bar in Triana. You must visit me there.'"

After the Boeing stabilized, I looked out of the window, watching a sea of clouds down below, knowing this trip was my only chance to discover the true story of Ganador's earlier life in Spain. After all, there must be a reason why Ganador had been sold from a Gypsies yard? King's do not live with Gypsies; neither do they work as guard horses in scrap yards. I had to find the truth.

And I swore that somehow I'd make sure I visited Pepe. I had to persuade Mum to take a walk by the river into Triana barrio. She loved the west side of the Guadalquivir, and Pepe's flamenco bar stood right there in Plaza del Altozano...

2. Fiesta

After the flight I rang Mum. "I'll be with you soon Mum…"

"Thank goodness for that…" The instant I heard her voice, I knew I'd done the right thing by travelling all this way.

On leaving departures I looked for dad, he always stood in the same spot just outside the entryway. With a sharp twinge I realized he would never be there again.

A taxi waited outside the airport, everything seemed brighter there, sounds of living, traffic, laughter. Sounds that dad would never hear anymore, a roadway full of things he'd never see again. Wiping away tears, I gave the driver directions to the flat.

Mum stood outside the entrance, she paid the driver, insisted on carrying my case and kissed my forehead the way she always did.

"Let's go inside love. You must need a cup of tea." Once in the flat, we sat on the sofa and talked, or mum talked. Everything she'd kept bottled up just spilled out. "Mind if we talk about dad?" Without waiting for a reply she unloaded her worries, powerless to stop herself.

"A Doctor was on hand immediately, saved his life … for a short time."

"Did we thank him?"

"The man didn't leave his name."

"So we can't thank him."

"Dad's yearly medical gave him the all clear. Do you know, I keep wondering if they made a mistake, or, if everything was done to save him?" She sounded defeated, as though life had suddenly lost its meaning.

How wrong I'd been in thinking Mum would go first, always the more delicate of the two. No-one can foretell the future, not even yearly medicals. When the clock strikes the hour, it doesn't matter if you're weak, strong, young or old.

Once Mr. D.N.A. has run out of code, times up… terminado.

"He'd come to the end of his life Mum."

"I suppose you're right."

That night in my bedroom I found solace in the tiniest detail, each item, every scratch. My room was kept exactly how I remembered, favorite books, old teddy bears, sketches, paintings. And then I saw something new. On the side wall was a picture of Ganador, the first print I'd proudly posted to Dad. Under the photo, he'd written these words:

'On his brow he carries the brilliant mark of the morning.' Horse of Kings 1295 Al Andaluz

Dad had been waiting to see Ganador, to gaze at his splendor, marvel at his air born movement. But all that was gone. Now I only had memories. I lay awake until early dawn thinking of the words under the photo … until drifting into exhausted sleep.

The following morning I accompanied Mum to Callé Sierpes, the main shopping street of Seville, and a paradise for rich shoppers, a place where smart designer shops stood side by side with expensive stores. Mum insisted on buying me a gorgeous hand worked wrap, she said, "we have to go somewhere special tonight, so you can wear the nice shawl. Think of it as a late birthday present."

"Would you like to walk by the river tonight, like we used to do?" I asked hopefully.

"There's nothing I'd like better," replied Mum, and I sighed with relief.

*

As the bell tower tolled the hour of ten, we strolled through Parque Maria De Louisa, on the east bank of the river Guadalquivir. In the distance, as far away as the wooded areas; I heard echoes of flamenco. Seville hummed with excitement after dark, especially on nights of Gypsy Festivals.

For a few minutes we sat on a park bench, and my thoughts strayed to Ganador's earlier life in Seville when he proudly pulled his masters carriage, along the side of the river, trotting in step with his brother Papillon. I thought of the tales Pepe had told me at the Romany wedding, a period of almost one year ago… but a moment in time that would live in my mind forever…

'Ganador was no ordinary carriage horse," Pepe had told me. "He was the finest Spanish horse in Sevilla. When the moon was full, the Masters greatest pleasure in life was to ride in his carriage through the old town. You see, Ganador and his brother Papillon were the finest driving pair in Spain. Always, he requested the same route … down past the beautiful gardens of the Alcazar, where the pair moved slowly and in step, almost piaffe, which gave the carriage an illusion of moving, but advancing little. Antonio wished to linger and dream of the past; he loved to watch the dancing lights on the Alcazar's walls. He called the golden glow, 'the sunlight of the night.'

After the Alcazar I would drive the carriage into Santa Cruz, through a warren of white alleyways, under flower filled balconies. Here, people crowded into the road, wanting to touch the horses for luck. I've seen crowds stand and applaud … I've seen grown men weep. Ganador loved those nights, he knew they were special. The stallion passaged all the way round the old town, head held high, so very proud to be serving his Master!

When the master gave the order to cross the bridge into Triana, Ganador always whinnied with delight. If I close my eyes, I can imagine the sounds of those nights, ringing hooves on cobbles, horses blowing. I can see garlands of flowers around their necks and glints of diamonds in their forelocks. Ganador was one of those rare horses who live for the moment. There was only one important item on Ganador's agenda, his wish to show off his Master, and the ovation of the crowd.

Late at night, with sounds of flamenco all around, I would drive into the Plaza and halt the carriage outside our flamenco tableaux.

Antonio claimed it was his favorite out of all Sevilla!

Ganador always drew a crowd of onlookers, he delighted in performing tricks. With his lips he opened handbags, snatched handkerchiefs and even removed wallets. I taught him a lot of tricks when he was just a foal. After Ganador's show I would drive the carriage away to a quiet area near the river. There were many artists by the river, strolling musicians, flamenco dancers, portrait artistes. I loved those nights away from the Peña…they were magical times.'

All these wonderful sights and sounds had once been Ganador's. He had stood by the Guadalquivir, in the early hours of the morning … seen hundreds of glowing lanterns casting tremulous shadows on its water. He had seen pleasure boats sailing down river, bedecked in glittering lights. Maybe, he'd listened to the same street guitarist playing Toledo or Bach, as I listened to now … or heard the same flamenco with its wild haunting cries?

Mum brought me back to earth when she said, "You're thinking of Ganador…"

"How can you tell?"

"The eyes, they take on a far-away look."

*

After our stroll, we queued for a tourist bus which headed to La Pueblo de Triana on the west side of the river, and then we strolled along bustling Callé Del Betis to 'Manolos Tavern,' one of Mums favorite cafes.

We sat on the terrace, under shimmering palms watching brightly lit ferries sailing past …. Moonlight glistened on the rippling water. I closed my eyes imagining the perfume of the sea, the rhythm of the waves. The Guadalquivir had a pulse all of its own, the kind you had to be on familiar terms with to recognize it was a distant echo of the ocean.

"Listen to the singing." Mum pointed to the east side of the river and the Alcazar, it was bathed in shafts of golden light. I heard a distant, unaccompanied voice echo from the cathedral.

"I think he's singing a Saeta." Keeping my eyes firmly closed, I concentrated on the man's inspired singing, a subtle balance between energy and musical form.

"Why do Saetas always remind me of Gregorian plainchant? There must be a link somewhere down the line..."

"There is," replied Mum, "early church music and the mode. Dad called the Saeta ... the song of the Orient."

Gypsy cantaors stood at regular intervals along the route of the procession, over the Puente de Triana and down the length of Callé Del Betis. As the statues approached, Saetas were passed from one voice to the next ... every interpretation pierced the chatter of the crowds, as each man described the sufferings of the Crucifixion.

A firework display followed the procession, setting the sky alight with vibrant color. The music was flamenco, pure and passionate. After the procession a young Romany guitarist played gay Sevillanas, the flamenco of Seville. He sat in a corner of the terrace, eyes closed as if in a different world. I will never forget his dazzling technique and wild haunting cries. When he sang, his voice seemed to glide from one note to the next, through minute intervals, which were smaller than any semitone. This was the sound of the East...mystical, exotic, and so very beautiful. I tried to work out the rhythm and melodic line, but found it impossible...

"Norma!" Mum nudged my elbow. "There's a gentleman here, and I do believe you know him..." I must have been dreaming, for unknown to me Pepe's unmistakable figure stood right there, on the terrace of Manolos.

"Hola Norma, buenas noches..." The sound of his voice was unique, inimitable. The spoken melody of the Gitano's of Seville, half sung, half spoken, nothing like the rhyming dialect of the Romanies back home in England. At any moment I half expected him to break into flamenco cante, just like he'd done at the Romany wedding...

"Hola Pepe!" Seeing him was like a bolt from the blue, especially tonight, when being with Mum was the most important item on my agenda. I wanted to say, 'where can we meet, I've been longing to talk about Ganador.' But I couldn't just barge in and spoil Mum's evening. "Mum…" I whispered. "This is Pepe, father of Evita."

"I am acquainted with Pepe," she replied. "He's my flamenco teacher. However, I'm not familiar with him in his role as Evita's father. The world's a very small place you know, especially the horse world." It was obvious Mum and Pepe were the best of friends. Mum was a born charmer, who worked on the simple theory that men liked to hear nice things about themselves, a presumption which seemed to work most of the time.

Pepe sat on the only other chair; he looked pleased to see mum and me. His obvious surprise, left me feeling happy, and, in a strange way rather special.

After he'd spoken to Mum I noticed a look of anxiety in his eyes, maybe he wondered why I hadn't contacted him about my trip to Triana. Perhaps he thought I was ashamed of his identity, of his race?

"Tell me about Ganador," he said. "He is still with you?"

"He's not going anywhere else. I promise!"

"Ganador's not the kind of horse to be passed around. Not many understand his ways."

"What do you mean, his ways?"

"The master called him the wildest horse in this universe."

"I suppose he is. But that's what makes him special."

"When can we celebrate Ganador and his owner!" he asked, his voice was rich and melodic. His words were almost melody.

"I'd love to see your flamenco bar," I replied. "Is it the same one you told me of, where Ganador stood outside entertaining passersby?"

"It's the same one I told you of, where the sounds of flower girls and flamenco guitars are the only sounds."

"I would like that…"

Pepe bowed low in his usual manner, hand over heart. He made the sign of the cross in the air. Before his parting embrace he handed me his card. It was shiny and black … gold edged and lettered.

"How beautiful…" Mum watched him turn away.

"You mean his card?"

"No, the man, he's a very special person," she nodded in a knowing way. "Look at all the gold he wears, and how the waiters are so deferential when he passes."

"I'd say he's incredibly rich."

"Do you know" said Mum thoughtfully, "I have never met a man with such a powerful personality. He makes me feel nervous even though he appears kind..."

"Pepe's exactly the type of man Dad warned me about, a gentleman and a charmer. Wonder what he's up to?" The head waiter stood at the entry holding a white albino donkey. Pepe took the reins from him, and the waiter bowed.

"He must have walked in the procession with his donkey. I wonder where he keeps the animal."

"Some of these buildings in Triana have stables at the back."

"I didn't know that." I watched him walking down the brightly lit callé with his donkey, in and out of crowds of tourists. Lots of people stopped to look back at Pepe. Perhaps Mum was right; maybe he was a very special person.

A waiter brought a bottle of champagne to our table, 'Compliments from Señor Pepe.' Next to the bottle he placed a small white card, on the front was a detailed drawing of La Giralda mosque tower, and on the back just three words... 'Hasta Luego Pepe.'

A little later, after we'd eaten, Mum told me she wanted to stay in Spain. I wasn't surprised when she said, "I'm not moving because Dads died...I love this part of Andalucia."

"I know you do."

"The sherry triangle and Seville ... are like paradise to me."

"But you will come to the farm for holidays Mum?"

"Of course I will. I love coming to the farm, there's nowhere more beautiful than Yorkshire's moors..." Mum hesitated, and then she said, "I've just one request..."

"Would you like the cottage next door as a holiday home?" I asked optimistically.

"What I'd like to do is put my favorite armchair in a big bay window and gaze out over the valley. Those tiny mullioned windows stop me dreaming."

What I didn't say was, 'prepare for a long wait as the farms a listed building…'

3 Plaza Del Altozano

After dinner, we strolled in the steps of Pepe and his donkey, into Seville's other world, the Romany enclave of Triana barrio. Once a closed society to the city's Gypsies, until a clash of cultures got in the way and the council moved most of the Gypsies out ... to flats in suburbia.

"I think he went down here..." We turned down a narrow callé lined with warehouses that mingled with up-market bars. "Been taken over by the arty set," Mum said knowingly. "These warehouses used to be homes."

Everything altered as we left the brightly lit riverside area, gone were the sounds of chatter and river boats, here the streets rang with the sounds of flower sellers, traders, and flamenco guitars.

"East and west of the Guadalquivir are like two different worlds. Some call Triana, the wild side! I'm just surprised they don't have guards on the bridges..."

In the warehouses lining the side road, tall windows showed off fine ceramic art. The displays were lit not by fluorescent lighting but by sparkling chandeliers. "Bet you don't recognize the new Triana."

After walking down a cobblestone alleyway, we entered a brightly lit square close to the river. The square was lined with original Gypsy houses, noisy flamenco bars and taverns. A carriage rattled past, it drew to a halt in front of a central fountain. I watched a girl run out from the shadows to meet the carriage. An important looking man stepped down; the girl lowered her head in obeisance, bobbed a curtsy and offered him a red rose. 'Just look,' said Mum, 'the horse knows the girl.' Fractiously, the horse whinnied and struck the cobbles until sparks flew. And the girl offered the horse sugar before escorting the man to a table.

My heart raced with excitement thinking I walked on the same cobbles that Ganador once trod. Maybe Evita had run out to welcome Ganador? It was difficult to believe that my Ganador at home in Yorkshire had once been a visitor to this square, and thought of as the finest carriage horse in Seville...

"This is what's left of the gypsy quarter, and it's where I come for my flamenco class! Can you feel the atmosphere?"

"Be difficult not to. It's electric! This square is like another world..."

The tapping of dancer's feet echoed from open windows, with steps so rapid I was aware of the whole and not the part. We passed African musicians playing oriental music using scale patterns I didn't recognize. I listened to brilliant cadenzas coming to rest in harmonies I had no knowledge of, dreamlike obscure. We passed dark skinned Gypsy women who moved with a type of elegance I'd never seen before. The women stared and then turned away, as if an unseen veil existed between my world and their own.

"Would you like to visit Pepe's bar now?" asked Mum.

"I can't wait," I said. "I can hardly believe my luck."

At the other side of the plaza we sat at a table outside the tavern. Pepe's tavern was bustling; men were standing everywhere, in the doorway and out onto the terrace.

"All the Gypsies in Triana must be here."

"How do you know they're all Gypsies?"

"I suppose it's the lack of females. Gypsy women usually stay home."

"I wonder why?" said Mum.

Inside the tavern I heard the solo voice of a man. He sang the opening bars of a Sevillanas, the flamenco of Seville. Every sound was precisely as I remembered at the Romany wedding, spontaneous, and full of passion. When Pepe stopped singing, the cante was passed round the room, then out onto the terrace. Every voice, young and old sang of the sorrows and joys of life, in a way that made their song unlike any flamenco I'd heard before.

"This is wonderful," I said. "I'll always remember tonight."

"Triana is where the legend of flamenco song was born."

"What do you mean? I never knew flamenco was steeped in myth and legend."

"In the Iglesia de Santa Ana, stands the gypsy font, which passes on the gift of flamenco song to the children of the faithful." Mum nodded towards the ancient church as she told the tales of some of Spain's greatest flamenco singers … most of who were born in Triana.

"What a lovely story."

"Faith's a wonderful thing," replied Mum sharply.

Out of the shadows, a darkly handsome Gypsy youth drifted over to our table. He paused, before holding out his hand.

"It's been a long time," he said softly. "How's me brave lad … how's me Ganador? Every hour of every day I've thought of the lad." Standing right next to me was Mark; the same Mark who'd been Ganador's inseparable partner at the Gypsy yard, the same Mark who informed me he'd never get over losing the horse. He looked at me steadily, in a way that reminded me his every word was true.

"And Ganador's missed you," I said truthfully. "He examines every man with jet black hair very carefully."

Mark shook his head sadly, "Not as much as I've missed him." There was no answer to that, better say nothing.

"Tell me about him," he asked wistfully. So I did just that, I told him every detail about Ganador's life on the moors, his daily routine, how the local villager's adored him, and just a few of his adventures. He laughed, and the brightness returned to his eyes, the same bright eyes I remembered as being the color of dark rich chocolate.

"So Ganador loves the moors…"

"He loves to roam and look at the world."

"The Romanies say 'the longing lies in the distance,' 'tis a Gypsy saying that means the oss likes the freedom of the open road. Likes watching sun, wind and earth become one…" Mark winked as Mum scribbled the timeless words of the Romanies into her diary. Mark hadn't changed at all; he looked exactly as I remembered him on the day of his wedding, charming, boyish and Gypsy through and through.

"And how's Evita?"

"She's fine. Evita loves Seville. She helps run Pepe's flamenco bars; it's what you call the family business so it is."

"Tell me how you met Evita," asked mum. "There must be a story waiting to be told…"

"There's a story alright," said Mark. "And sometimes I still can't believe she's there…can't believe I was so lucky."

4 'Mark's Story'

We followed Mark under a tableaux sign, then down a cobbled path where olive trees shimmered silver in the moonlight. At the back of the tavern, tables and chairs were set out on a terrace overlooking the Guadalquivir. I stopped and listened to the sounds of flamenco coming and going on the warm spring air, sounds of clapping and tapping that merged and became one with the distant echo of river boats sailing downstream...

He opened a door marked 'Privado,' and turned on a light.

Glistening Spanish antiques lined the walls, soft velvet chairs stood invitingly around coffee tables.

"Chiffoniers" said mum; she nodded to the ornate black furniture, "must be where they entertain." For a few minutes Mark disappeared from the room, when he returned he carried a pot of fresh coffee.

"So you want to hear the tale of Evita?" Mark paused for a moment, and then his words just spilled out...

'When Ganador had been with us for three months, just long enough for him to get to know us, and us to know him, the head groom from the mansion came to the yard. He carried an important looking envelope in his hand, stamped with Sir Roland's coat of arms it was. The instant mother saw him, she ran to get Dad and me. Crying she was.

"Roland wants the horse sold," Dickens said sadly, "believes he's an embarrassment to him."

"What do you mean?" I asked.

"Doesn't want him stabled here any longer, thinks his friends might find out..."

"Find out what?"

"That he's stabled with Gypsies. Wants him sold and moved as far away as possible, that's what Roland says. And I don't like bringing bad news. I'm sorry lad."

So I opened the letter and read it out to Dad, as he can't read small type. Mother didn't want to hear, she adored the oss. I could hear her sobbing from the other side of the yard.

Dear Adams,

I hereby authorize you to sell Ganador a.s.a.p. The stallion has damaged my reputation, my pocket and almost killed my wife. Sadly, I cannot trust the horse any longer.

If Ganador fails to sell at Appleby Fair, I instruct you to act as vendor and sell him at auction. Never will I accept Ganador back into my stables. As to price, a stallion of his stamp must be worth £3000 to any Gypsy, without any breed papers.

Roland R.

"Our time with Ganador seems to be running out Dad." I felt miserable I did, we'd all grown to love the oss in different ways, like a friend he was to mother. "What can we do?"

"I'll tell you what we'll do son, we'll do just what he orders. Take Ganador up to Appleby and give Sir Roland a run for his money. Price the oss high son, so no-one can buy him. But what we won't do is put Ganador into any auction. We'll look out for some nice people who'll give the oss a chance, so we will."

"So we're taking Ganador to the fair?"

"That's right son. We'll go through the motions and then do nothing, until Roland brings in his fancy solicitors, and he won't do that in a hurry."

And Dad sent me up to the mansion to ask his lordship for three hundred pounds. "Enough to pay for a little holiday son!"

So we did as we were ordered, we took Ganador up to Cumbria for the start of the fair. Appleby fair begins on the first Thursday after the first Tuesday in June. It's where we travelling people meet up to exchange gossip, trade an oss, or just do nothing at all. You will see gypsies, travelers, palm readers and Romanies. But, you will never see a more colorful horse fair than Appleby. Tis like a tale from old history, and taken place ever since the reign of James 11, who granted it a royal charter in 1685.

The fairs held at the highest point of Gallows hill, and spills out onto surrounding meadows. Gallows hill leads from the main street up to the fair, and is so named after public hangings. More than twenty hangings a month were carried out on that hill, with scaffolds standing waiting from bottom to top.

When we arrived, dad parked up close to the Romany area, away from the crowds and noise. The first thing he did was fasten a silver bell to Ganador's halter.

"Invisible," he said, "when under his mane." He ordered me to sleep with the caravan door open. "You must listen to the sound of Ganador's tinkling bell son." Before he went to the pub, he arranged a circle of fairy lights round our plot. "So folks can see he's watched over."

On that first night, I groomed Ganador, cleaned tack and polished his hooves until they shone. When I could do no more I sat in the caravan watching Romany men lighting fires for roasting lamb. You see, Romany men don't go to the pub at night, they keep to themselves, and they're worlds apart from Gypsies. They make money by trading gold and fine china … not osses.

So there I was feeling bored, when I saw a girl standing over by Ganador. I'd a feeling she may be one of our neighbors. The palm reader told dad that the family in the next wagon travel to Appleby each year for a holiday, and come all the way from Seville.

"My names Evita," the girl said, her accent was definitely foreign and she carried a bag of carrots for Ganador.

"I'm Mark…" She never answered, probably can't understand the lingo. At that moment I heard her say 'Ganador,' and then she said his name again. Sounded a bit different to the way I say it, but then she had a foreign accent.

"How do you know his name?" I asked. She just stared at me and carried on feeding him carrots. I watched her plaiting his forelock and laughing at his antics, she seemed to have a way with him. When she smiled, it was like the sun coming out, she has a lovely smile. At that moment, I felt myself melting, it's the only way I can describe the feeling. I never knew that falling for a girl felt like this.

"Will you eat with us tonight?" She held up both hands and counted up to ten, just for if I couldn't understand. From the first time we met, we understood each other. We seemed to read each other's minds. Like telepathy it was.

"Thank you," I said. "I'd like that."

Her mother walked close behind, pretending to look at a book whilst keeping a close eye on her. Romany girls are never left unaccompanied with a man, not until the day they wed.

"Evita only has a little English," her chaperone said. "But I speak good English."

"I'm glad to hear that."

"My names Mariapi, I'm Evita's mother."

"You look more like sisters so you do."

"Now you try to charm me!" with every movement of her body she opened and closed her fan, she's a beautiful woman. "Evita and her father Pepe know the stallion well." I'm feeling confused now, but don't want to show myself up by asking silly questions. "You must be wondering how we know Ganador?" And I just had to ask…

"I don't mean to be rude, but you do seem to be well acquainted with Ganador's past." Mariapi smiled at my ignorance and closed her fan with a snap.

"Ganador pulled the Masters carriage," she said ever so demurely.

"So Ganador pulled a carriage? Wait till I tell Dad, he'll never believe me."

"He was no ordinary carriage horse," she pointed out. "Ganador was the finest carriage horse in Sevilla."

"Thank you," I said. "I'm not familiar with Ganador's past."

"How can you be?" And the pair turned and walked away.

When I told Dad, he looked astonished … and then he started to laugh. "Shows how much Roland knows about osses son," he said with a chuckle. "Just imagine paying us to break the 'finest carriage horse in Sevilla' to harness!" And we laughed so much the caravan rolled about...

After that first meeting I sat with the Romanies every night. You see, dad was never there at night-time, he lived in Appleby's ale houses with his friends, telling them stories about Ganador, and spending Roland's money.

The Romanies made everything seem right about the world, and it was the only way I could be with Evita. At the feast there was music and dancing, time for singing. To begin, the melodies were played softly, just a violin and flute. Later, Pepe played flamenco guitar, he played a kind of music I'd never heard before, thrilling he was.

"Is this music Spanish?" I asked. Everyone laughed at my lack of knowledge, and I'd vowed not to say anything silly.

"You have never heard the music of Andalucia?" said Mariapi. "Then we must remedy that."

I remember watching Evita dance, she moved like I'd never seen before. I felt hypnotized by the passion of the music, and possessed by Evita.

*

Early the next morning I rode Ganador down to the riverside to wash his mane and tail. It's peaceful before the day begins, becomes too rough later. After washing him sparkling clean, I walked him down to the deep water where I put him on a long line. Ganador had no fear of deep water; he loved swimming against the current and plunging off the river bank into the water. People sitting outside the cafes gave him a round of applause and came to stand on the bridge. The instant Ganador saw crowds watching him ... he scrambled out of the river and plunged in again! How he loves to show off!

When I arrived back, I saw dad was deep in conversation with some stranger in uniform. After putting Ganador on his tether I walked over to see what was wrong.

"Where did you get the horse from Sir?" asked the policeman, he pointed to Ganador. "He's not a Gypsy horse. Can I see his papers?"

Dad just nodded, he'd never grovel to any policeman. The only thing that concerned dad was making a good impression on his drinking mates.

"Get the papers son," dad said, "they're under the mattress so they are." By now a small crowd had gathered, no-one was missing the drama of dad versus the law. Following his tales in the pub the night before, dad had become a celebrity, and so had Ganador.

"You can look all you want, so you can," said dad as he handed the letter over to the policeman. The crowd jeered at the poor man, who hurriedly scanned the letter.

"Everything seems to be in order Sir." The man scribbled something in his book and got out of the way quickly. Swallowed up by the crowd he was.

"Get the oss onto sellers run fast lad," dad said happily. "Looks a picture so he does, and tie this red ribbon in his tail, let them think he's a kicker."

"But I thought we're only going through the motions?"

"So we are. It's just for exercise son." I led Ganador down the run, he would only passage, felt like dynamite he did. When the crowd saw Ganador leaping about, they gathered around the run, cheering and clapping they were, prodding his ribs, feeling his legs, looking to find blemishes.

"Any man touching this oss does so at his own peril!" Dad pointed to the red ribbon in his tail and every one of the men scrambled back under the rope barrier.

Just then a rough looking dealer stepped forward. He raised his right hand, the sign of a potential buyer.

"Where did this oss come from Adams?" the dealer shouted, "tis not your type man…"

"A Spanish King!" replied dad. "Look at his finely boned head, feel his silken mane. There's never lived an oss so magnificent." All around was excitement and noise, enough to cause Ganador to explode, frightening he was.

The dealer pulled dads arm, a signal to start bartering.

"How much money's in your pocket man?" Dad spoke to the

crowd, not the dealer. They loved his mocking style. "Or did I forget to state his price?"

"You did, you did!!!" The crowd roared, they believed every word dad said.

"Well we might do business if you show me your money. That's if we start at £5000..." The moment he heard the price the dealer fled. Never saw him again.

Behind all the color and gaiety, horse fairs are a sad affair. If a dealers short of cash for beer or cards, he trots the oss he's just bought down sellers run, hoping to get his money back, plus fifty quid. Osses are sold many times in the course of the fair. Nothing but a piece of wood they are, to be knocked into shape and sold again at a profit. Look into the eyes of the creatures bought and sold by Gypsy dealers. You see a look of misery.

As the first trading day wore slowly to its end; a quiet descended over the fair. For a few hours the horses could graze peacefully, if no rough youths upset them with fireworks.

Tonight's Saturday, it's the most important get together for the men; and the night Appleby's ale houses are full inside and out. After taking Ganador for a walk, I groomed him, cut some lush grass from under the hedgerow and filled up his hay net. Only when I'd finished all the jobs did I allow myself to think about Evita, the way she touched my hand, how she looked deep into my eyes.

At ten, I watched Romany men lighting fires for cooking, and the women preparing food. The music was of a Spanish guitar and distant chattering voices. After feeding Ganador I fastened the silver bell to his halter, turned on the fairy lights and made my way over to the Romany area.

Mist was hovering over the river as I walked across the meadow and ribbons of blue smoke swirled over Appleby. Everything was perfect that night. When Evita came out of the wagon, we sat together looking into the fire. I placed my arm around her shoulders for I could sense she wanted to lay her head close to mine. But then I saw Mariapi watching, so we had to draw apart. Dad doesn't know about Evita, not yet. Although I've a feeling he's going to know very shortly.

Once the food was cleared away, Mariapi came over; she kissed me on both cheeks, embraced me and said something really strange. "We'll have to work something out." Maybe Evita's told her she loves me? If so, there will be a meeting with dad, when he's not in the pub that is. After the feast Evita told me her age. She scraped one and three into the remains of the ashes…

Early the following morning, dad walked over to Evita's stall, just as she was setting out china ornaments. Her family trade in gold, jewelry, and fine hand painted china. The paintings on the china portrayed English country lanes, Peddlers wagons and high stepping horses, all white, all identical to Ganador. Evita told me the art work was carried out by 'the Gypsies of Triana.'

Dad only wanted a trinket for mother, something nice to take home. Mother refuses to visit fairs - she can't bear to see horses treated roughly. Just as Evita's wrapping the gift, Mariapi walked over and took dad's arm. She leaned over to whisper in his ear and invites him into their living wagon. A full ten minutes later dad walks back; he's smiling and tapping his boot with his riding crop.

"You've done well for yourself son … Marrying into money so you are!" I breathed a sigh of relief, at last I know Evita's mine…

*

Saturday's the busiest trading day of the fair, crowds were gathering as early as eight a.m. There looked to be hundreds walking up gallows hill, never seen the fair so hectic. Dad wants me to run Ganador out in the afternoon, 'just to show him off son.' Never crosses dad's mind that the showground's too noisy for the likes of Ganador. The oss can't bear shouting and loud music. Neither does he like straying fingers touching him. When the time arrived for trotting him down sellers run, Ganador's in a real panic. Leaping in the air he was and rearing almost vertical. Dad's drinking mates don't make handling him any easier with all the clapping and cheering they do.

It's then I saw a flashy looking type of gent shaking dad's hand,

and watching Ganador, must have pushed his way through the crowd.

"He's a well bred horse if ever I saw one." The man looked at Ganador's teeth and stroked his mane. "Like a fall of silk..." This man's no Gypsy, he's filthy rich, and I worry about how wealthy he really is. If there's good profit to be made, I think dad will sell Ganador, even though he promised he'd never sell him. I wish I could trust dad, but I can't. Not where there's money to be made.

"You have money to spend and can see fine breeding Sir." I can read dad's mind, he's imagining stacks of money.

"I am looking to buy class horses for use in films. He would carry a King!" As he said 'King,' the man lifted his arm to point to Ganador. The oss went into a frenzy of plunging and rearing, his front legs were thrashing the air.

"This oss was owned by a King!" shouts dad, he's playing to the crowd and he's in front of a live audience of men who buy his beer, who think he's a hero. Suddenly, the film man pulled dad's arm and said, 'tell me his price." The crowd's going wild, just waiting for the bidding to begin. So guess what dad said? He raised the price yet again so he did...

"The oss is £10, 000 and cheap at that!"

"My top bid is £9, 000," the film man shouts. To think Sir Roland told dad to sell at three thousand, and now he's refusing nine?

Just then I saw Pepe push through the crowd, he walked right over to dad's box, so he stood between dad and the city gent.

"To sell Ganador to any film man would break Evita's heart," said Pepe. He spoke in a loud clear voice, in a tone that silenced the crowd.

Trouble is, I can see dad's tempted, his face is purple. But Pepe's warning as to the consequences put a stop to any thoughts of making money out of Ganador.

"Take him back Mark," dad shouts to the crowd. "This man has been wasting our time." And the crowd jeered at the well dressed man who was quickly gone. When dad stood down from his wooden box, he and Pepe shook hands. Some of dad's drinking mates thought he'd sold Ganador to Pepe, and began to cheer. But they dare not ask, for there are two rules never discussed in the travelling world, a man's financial transactions, and dowries ... and dad wasn't about to give anything away.

On Sunday the weather turned wet, clouds were gathering and the rain formed a fog on the caravan windows. Something special's happening tonight, Mariapi and Pepe have invited dad and me for drinks in their living wagon.

Before we go, dad examined my neckties. He chose the red silk scarf from Dublin's horse fair, it's my favorite.

"Dress in your finery son!" he handed me his gold bracelet together with a pair of shiny black dealer boots he'd bought that very morning in Appleby. Dad got dressed up too. He wore his American style boots with an emerald green suit and lots of gold. As I tied the scarf he walked over and sat at the opposite side of the table.

"And don't forget to give her this necktie!" He leaned forwards and looked at me with his razor sharp eyes. When he bent towards me, I noticed he'd greased his thinning hair down, so it covered his bald patch, and he never does that, except on important occasions. "Tie the scarf neatly son," he said. "It means everything. Like an engagement ring it is."

"When should I give it to Evita dad?"

"Hand the scarf over when we're all sitting together."

Later, whilst we sat having drinks, I passed the silk necktie across the table, so it lay in front of Evita. Everybody fell silent. My whole life depends on whether she accepted this token. I was shaking with nerves.

For a few moments she just stared at the red scarf ... I knew dad was worried by the way he tapped his foot, maddening it was. Then, just as I thought my worst fear had come true, she bowed her head and began to cry. Not loud and gushing, but quietly.

Mariapi laid her hand on Evita's arm, just to let her know her mother was with her.

"You must ask yourself what you want to do," she said. "You must listen to your heart child."

With her eyes closed, Evita placed her hand on the table, and searched for a corner of the necktie. Right at that moment the summer storm broke and a deluge of rain fell, sounded like thundering on the wagons roof. No-one knew what to do, so we all looked up, as if the rain might suddenly pour in.

Whilst the parents were busy looking up at the ceiling, I stretched out my hand to touch hers.

"I love you," I whispered. And then, everything happened! She gave me a little smile, picked up the scarf, and put it to her lips! She wrapped it round her head to hold back her hair! Everyone in the wagon stood up to clap, and for the first time I was allowed to hold her hand...

"The date of the wedding will be fixed tonight." Dad whispered in my ear. "Maybe one month, could be two, but then I don't know the laws with Spanish Romanies ..."

"What will mother say?"

"She'll say you've done well for yourself son..."

The downpour began later that night. In the morning the show field was changed from a firm green meadow into grey slush.

"What's finished is finished," grumbled dad. "Best away before the wagon sinks." So we drove down Gallows hill into the road lined with coffee shops and overhanging trees. The once peaceful river was surging high and swollen, neither man nor horse could have survived its violence.

As soon as we pulled into the scrap yard, Mother came running to the gate.

"Has Ganador gone away?" she asked anxiously.

"Ganador's here Mother ... No-one had the money to buy our Ganador!" And she stared through a peep hole in the grooms' door. You should have seen her face light up...'

"And when did you next see Evita?" I asked.

"Because of Pepe's flamenco bars, the wedding had to be delayed for almost a year. When I next saw Evita was the following year at Appleby fair. I will always remember her jumping out of Pepe's wagon and looking for Ganador ... she looked for him before she spoke to me!"

"Where's Ganador?" she cried. And I had to tell her that Ganador had been sold. She was very upset and for a time I thought the wedding would be called off.

"I wanted to see Ganador more than anything in this world," she sounded so sad. "Ganador's to be my holy horse at 'our' wedding."

When I told Dad what she'd said he promised Ganador would be Evita's holy horse. And somehow, he arranged for Ganador to pay us a visit...

"That was a lovely story," said Mum. "Who would have thought that Ganador brought you and Evita together?"

5 'Pepe's Story'

"Will there be time to meet tomorrow?" Mark asked worriedly. "Pepe had to return to the stables, there's a problem with a mare. Pepe always makes sure the horses are looked to…"

"Someone has to. It's a good thing he's so caring." We shook hands in the way of the Romanies, thumbs on top, elbows touching. "I'd love to accept the invitation … if Mum agrees."

The following evening I went to meet Pepe alone. Mum said her feet ached after all the walking, so I left her relaxing and made my way to the square in a taxi. Mark showed me to a different part of the casa, down some stairs and along a corridor.

"Pepe's study," he said opening the door to a cozy room. "While you're waiting, take a look at his books. Pepe's something of a hoarder, so he is."

"Before you go I've a question. Pepe calls himself head groom, but somehow I can't believe him."

Mark laughed. "He's part owner of the Yeguada where Ganador was bred and raised. Calls himself head groom, but the titles for the hacienda if you ask me."

A tall bookcase stood on the wall behind his desk; it was lined with leather bound works on Spanish history and warfare. Very carefully I opened the book standing closest to me. It was very old and fragile, amongst its contents were scenes portraying mounted warfare. On the page where the book fell open I read these words:

*

'The Iberian combat troops are unrivalled in the history of our civilization-they are hardy and tough and both man and horse can exist on the most frugal of diets. It is their incorrigible strength of spirit that gives them great superiority in battle. Horse and man are brought up to fight, and fighting is their duty, crusading in their blood. Both horse and man are a professional fighting force. A force wanted by every country...'

Somewhere near the back of the old book I read some more, about the savagery of combat:

'The Iberian warriors train their horses to fight by practicing movements used in battle and then repeating the actions of combat until perfect. The clever battle horses quickly learn to obey the sudden movements of combat and to protect their Master at any cost, striking and savaging the enemy when on the ground. Dogs too are used to fight the enemy; they are protected by spiked coats of armor to guard them from flying arrows. The difference in temperament between the combat horse and the working horse cannot be compared...'

*

Removing pen and book from my pocket I quickly scribbled the words down. Whoever had written this account had a thorough knowledge regarding the philosophy of early warfare, and more than a little understanding of horse and rider. And the only scribe to fit into that category was Xenophon, 369 B.C. or thereabouts. At the back of the old book was a page with strange words and symbols, nothing I could understand. Holding the book gave me a feeling close to that of finding a secret room filled with hidden treasure. I was reading the history of the ancient Spanish horse and warrior ... from the pen of a man who had observed and studied Iberian combat with its singularly unique style of attack. A man who must have watched the training and day to day life of warriors preparing for battle and their protectors, the earliest and fiercest combat horses ever bred, a force wanted by every country.

"Well!" I said in surprise. "These accounts say it all...wonder who wrote them?" When I turned round I found that Mark had gone. Placing the book back on the shelf, I gazed upwards and saw three photos on top of the bookcase. The first and third portrayed a woman holding a fan, and I felt sure the photos were of Mariapi. The middle image showed a carriage and pair standing in front of a castle. Feeling as if an intruder, I walked round the room studying the art work on display.

Tapestry's covered the remaining walls with scenes depicting fine horses and high mountains.

Just then I heard his voice, "Bought it in Morocco," he said, pointing to the largest tapestry. 'A Berber tribe were selling off their tents and worldly possessions, told me they'd no alternative but to find work and give up nomadic life. '

"Is the horse Berber? I thought the breed was extinct."

"The horse depicts a famous Berber stallion, believed to trace back to the times of Tarik ibn Ziyad, the Berber warrior who headed the Muslim invasion of Spain…His blood lines are somewhere in eastern Europe."

"And the mountain is Gibraltar?"

"Yes," he said correcting my pronunciation. "It's the mountain of Tarik … Jebel Tarik. But we talk of Ganador, not history. I know you want to hear Ganador's story." We sat down. Pepe behind his desk and me opposite…

"Please tell me about him …" I asked.

"Ganador was no earthly horse," he said quietly. "He carried the spirit of his ancestors, the horse of King's. He should never have been sent away for breaking … and it was wrong to sell him to England."

"Why do you say it was wrong to sell him to England?"

"Selling Ganador to England lost Spain one of its oldest bloodlines, a line that's almost extinct. His ancestors were bred to fight, and it's easy to mistake bravery with temper. When he was but a young horse, some thought him dangerous, and not many got on with him. Ganador lives in a different world to any English horse, to any normal horse."

"What do you mean dangerous?"

"Ganador was bred from the bravest lines of fighting horses ever to have lived, and when a highly bred stallion loses its trust in man, it is possible for wild instincts to take over. And from time to time, a horse turns into a rebel; always looking for the next fight. Horses don't think like we do. There's a very fine line between fight and flight, and when something terrible happens to a horse, especially a stallion like Ganador, that line becomes even finer, until it's blurred, and then, he might suddenly turn violent… If Antonio had kept him at home to be broken quietly, things would have been different."

"So it didn't work out?"

"No," he said sadly. "Things didn't work out."

"If you want to tell me what happened… whatever it is won't stop me loving him…"

"When Ganador had been at the breakers for one week, I decided to visit him. What I first noticed was the sadness in his eyes. I took a carrot from my pocket and held it for him to chew. As he nudged me with his nose, I noticed a ring of tiny scars around his nostrils, the sign of force from a metal nose band.

'My poor Ganador,' I said scratching his nose. 'The brutes giving you pain.' A groom overheard me, only a boy, but full of his own importance.

'He's not trained in manners,' the boy whined. 'Types like him are better with a bullet.'

'And what do you know of the ways of stallion's boy?'

'José tells me the ways of stallions. And he knows.'

'Then you'd better tell me what he knows.'

'A good horse should be like a good woman … quiet and submissive. If it has spirit, break it. That's what he says…'

After a few days I visited the yard again. This time, I stayed out of sight. There was a tall gateway on the side of the arena, where horseboxes pulled in. A good place to hide if I wished to see what was going on."

"How old was Ganador?"

"He was only a colt, two years and six months."

"What did you see?"

"The trainer walked behind Ganador holding long reins to a

sereta noseband. To my horror he attached a check rein, to keep his head up high. Can you imagine the pain when Ganador found it impossible to lower his head? The horse shone wet with sweat almost immediately."

"What happened then?"

"The bully whipped him into piaffe and passage, no warming up, he tired the horse out."

"Did Ganador retaliate?"

"Oh yes. Ganador hit back. Arching his neck, he tried to run, but his weary hind legs refused to carry him. So he did what came naturally ... he leapt into the air and snapped the reins. He put up a fearsome fight, plunging and rearing. He pounded the air with his forefeet, and then he charged at his torturers, José and the boy. And I believe he injured the boy. I ran through the stables and onto the arena, 'drop the whip man,' I ordered, and wrenched the weapon from him. But the fool stood there, he was shouting, 'I'll break his spirit...' Of course, José didn't comprehend that Ganador was prepared to die on that arena rather than allow any man to break his spirit. Ganador's spirit would never be broken ... Not until he takes his last breath. His forefathers were the fiercest combat horses in the world. Horses like Ganador do not understand fear, neither are they aware of submission, and there was no way José could ever win. Not now. Not ever.

On that arena, Ganador's trust in man had come to end. His experience had taught him he was far stronger than any man. Ganador would never be completely safe again...

That night, I told Antonio about Ganador's rough treatment and my plan to remove the two horses."

"He is to have no more torture," Antonio said. "What's happened is through my greed, my stupid wish to win Sevilla's pair driving championship with Ganador and Papillon ... and look what I've done..."

"Maybe I can have them ready in time," I said. "But on one condition."

"What's the condition?"

"That Ganador be sold afterwards..."

"Why?" asked Antonio. "Ganador's my favorite stallion."

"Your wellbeing," I replied. "When a stallion of Ganador's lineage learns he's stronger than a man... he can become dangerous."

"Did he become dangerous?" I asked.

"He was always on guard and only one groom was allowed to enter his box. Never stopped patrolling, traumatized he was."

"Did you prepare the horses in time for the championship?"

"Yes. I found ways of calming Ganador. Not always fool proof, but better than nothing. When the pair returned home, I made sure Papillon was always beside Ganador. In the carriage and in the stable the two were at all times together. He needed to know his brother was right there."

"What happened after the championship?"

"We received an offer from an English gentleman, for the pair. After his visit, the man arranged for Ganador and Papillon to travel to England."

"And did you see him again?"

"The next time I saw Ganador would be at Appleby fair in seventy eight. The moment I saw him at the fair, I knew he'd come to the bottom of the owners' ladder. Right down to the floor. Stallions with temperaments like Ganador usually do."

The instant Pepe said Appleby fair; I remembered the day back in seventy eight when Geoff had said, 'fancy a drive up to Appleby?' It was the second Tuesday in June ... a day of early summer warmth, too lovely to stay home. The fair was in full swing when we arrived. We watched colored horses being groomed by the riverside, before walking up Gallows hill to the selling area.

I remembered the mystery stallion I'd seen at the fair, the stallion's temperament of fire and his stunning beauty. We stood behind the rope barrier on seller's run, and though I could only see the stallion from a distance, I knew he was very handsome ... I also loved his color, it was shining silver.

And I thought of the boy who handled the stallion. How he put the other men to shame with his fearless way of handling the spirited creature. Whatever the horse did, the boy would be at his side, whispering, cajoling but always fearless and forever his friend. The frightened horse trusted the boy and the boy loved the horse … and that boy had been Mark … and the horse … Ganador.

"Following Appleby," said Pepe, "the next time I saw Ganador was on the day you brought him to Evita's wedding. The happiest day of my life it was, seeing Evita happy and content. Having Ganador as holy horse meant everything to the girl. She loved the horse and it broke her heart when he was sold."

"And now… I love Ganador," I whispered. And Pepe touched my hand and spoke so very low, his voice filled with emotion.

"You must always remember that the remainder of Ganador's story lies with you," said Pepe. "And I hope it's happier than his past."

I felt overwhelmed as I thought of all what the stallion had been through. Ganador did not understand present day man; his spirit was fired by the wild courage of his ancestor's, carried down to him through the bravest blood of fighting horses.

"No wonder he's the wildest horse in the Universe…" I said.

Pepe smiled at my comment and started to sing, a melody line that quickly developed into flamenco cante. I was sure he sang of Ganador…

6 'Excitement In The Square…'

Later that night there was a feeling of excitement in the square. Something different was about to happen, I felt the atmosphere change … from enjoyment to anticipation.

"Follow me," said Mark. "Two lads from the bullring have a score to settle…could be a wild one!"

Mark led the way across the cobbled square to a pathway that lay between a Peña and shadows. The path sloped gently downwards to a clearing close to the river. A circle had been flattened in the middle of the clearing, maybe larger than a circus ring, topped with newly raked sawdust, and surrounded by rushes. Where the rushes ended sailing boats swayed in rhythm with the tide and endless ripples lapped the shore.

"A natural harbor," said Mark, "Pepe's boat is the one with white sails, uses it for entertaining he does."

Just then I noticed a steady stream of Gypsies strolling down the path, men from the squares taverns. They stood in groups around the clearing, possibly placing bets with men who repeatedly shouted odds and waved their arms about. Were they bookies? In the space of a few minutes the mood had changed from peaceful to lively, and I began to feel worried.

"What happens now?" I asked, watching a man push past carrying a sword. "Perhaps I should have stayed home with mother. I don't understand what's going on."

"A dual," Mark said happily.

"What happens in this dual? What does the winner have to do?"

"Unseat his opponent! And I'm betting on the bay." Removing his wallet he counted out a thick wad of peseta notes. "Six to four

41

on," he said cheerfully. "So you have never seen a dual?"

"Only one," I said, "and that was at Golega horse fair. I seem to have forgotten the name…"

"Dual of the white arms," he replied quickly. "They know how to keep tradition alive over here."

At that moment the first horseman entered the arena. In his left hand he held the reins plus a white shield, whilst in his right he carried a counter balanced lance. The bay took position in the center of the clearing; angrily it struck the ground and began screaming out stallion calls. Never had I seen such a look of wild courage in the eyes of any horse. Until now…

And then, the man held up his hand as though to silence the crowd. His voice pierced the air as he shouted the ancient battle cry of the Iberian warrior:

'Who will fight me in mortal combat?'

His words echoed round the clearing, and there was total silence. Right at that moment a second horseman hurtled into the ring; he rode a black stallion that answered the bay with piercingly angry shrieks. From the first few minutes it became obvious the stallions before me were bred from the old lines, for their courage and fighting abilities…

Swerving to a halt the second horseman shouted:

"I will fight you in single combat…"

A drum roll started up somewhere in the distance, the sound set me on edge and I felt chilled to the core. But surely this was a re-enactment of what used to happen? The din was deafening as the two men fenced. Each blow meeting the full force of his opponents lance. Each man sought to take advantage of the other, so as to catch him unawares. The fencing passed rapidly from attacked to attacker and vice versa. Obedience without reserve was called for, instant obedience, in which the horses became strangely excited, showing brilliant piaffe and passage.

Suddenly, the black stallion plunged at the bay. Or did he plunge at the bays rider? Striking out with his teeth, he missed the man, opening up a gash on the bays wither. All the men around began to shout and jeer. Now I knew what it must have felt like to live in Roman times. Did I sense the same primitive thrill of excitement that the crowds felt in prehistoric days, in an era when mounted duals were a popular part of any entertainment?

Unexpectedly, the riders threw down their lances and the horses galloped round the ring. The bay moved alongside the black, and with one swift push its rider knocked his opponent out of the saddle. But the fight didn't end there, the bays rider leapt down to the ground, and then drew his short sword.

The two men fought the last part of the dual on foot. There was no holding back now ... the men struck or parried with swords or kicks. The fight ended when the black stallions' rider fell to the ground... the winner's sword across his throat.

"Nothing to worry about," said Mark, "the weapons are blunted."

"Even so ... it's been a shocking reminder of what Iberian horses were bred for."

"The fencing match between two mounted warriors was the normal way to fight in Iberia; it put the Iberian horse streets ahead of any other breed!"

"And gave a whole new meaning to the rough and tumble of the battlefield," I said thoughtfully. From what I had seen tonight, the mounted dual needed practiced riders who rode with stirrups, for without stirrups and a rounded knee, it was impossible to handle the lance with any degree of precision. It also required horses which possessed extreme agility and more than a little training, all of which, pointed to one very interesting fact. That the rough outlines of classical riding were laid down at this point in history, ready to be further developed when the Spanish horse was not used solely for survival ... but used for pleasure. And a new art form was born, the earliest ideology of classical riding... as long ago as pre history.

As Mark collected his winnings, a Gypsy woman took my eye. At least four youths were handing over wads of money, which she placed in a shopping bag. When all the money was stacked in the bag, she zipped it up tightly.

"What's she doing?" I asked Mark, pointing to the woman.

"Professional gamblers," he said watching her hand out cards.

"Giving the lads her next bet … with the odds she wants. They're probably off to the dog racing."

"Does she always win?"

"Not always, but she wins more than she loses."

After a few minutes, the clearing became peaceful, horses and men returning to their respective dwelling or drinking place. As I prepared to leave I heard the sound of distant hoof beats becoming louder…

Then, with an explosion of energy a young man wearing jeans, jumper and top hat cantered a Spanish horse into the arena, it was golden colored and very handsome.

"The horse is from Ganador's lineage, he's ridden down from the salon." Mark said proudly.

"I'm just glad it's not another fight."

The rider, a mere boy, leaned forwards and the horse took off at full gallop. I could see he rode without stirrups or saddle, just a snaffle bridle and sheepskin pad. There was an extraordinary sense of unity between man and horse, so much so I could imagine what it felt like to gaze at a centaur.

The boy-horse unit came to a sliding stop and bowed right in front of me. Unexpectedly, he began riding a high school routine. It was spontaneous and filled with energy, qualities only a master trainer would know how to achieve …

Many of the airs were based on natural movements, the same jumps and twirls I'd seen Ganador displaying as he played on the meadow.

He finished the display with movements originating in early combat … movements that had made the Iberian horse feared in battle, and wanted by every country.

There was something about the horse that brought back memories, but of what and who I could not recollect. And then I remembered! It was the day I spent with the master, Nuno Oliveira, the day I watched him displaying a golden colored stallion that lifted its legs very high and moved with a quality of other worldly brilliance I had never known possible.

"I think I know the horse," I whispered to Mark. "Nuno rode

him only last year."

"You could be right," he replied in a non-committal way. "High school riders seem to be on familiar terms with each other. Theirs is a very small world."

"Where does he perform?"

"He performs at the Salon, sometimes the Cirque de Paris and occasionally Sevilla Feria."

The boy and horse stood at a halt. He held the reins in his left hand, the velvet top hat in his right. On the stallions left flank was a brand - a crown and script written S, the same marking as that of Ganador. And at that moment, I understood some of the mystery surrounding Ganador. Pepe and his partner Antonio had to be 'aficionados' of the old line of Spanish Horse, one of the handful of breeders who still kept horses from Baroque lines.

"Why not ask him," said Mark. "He's a friend of mine."

As if in a dream, I walked over to his slim figure and thanked him for his wonderful display.

"Can I ask about your horse, his origins and trainer?"

"I made a promise never to disclose the name of his trainer," said the boy. "Why do you ask?"

"Because I have a stallion with the same brand," I mumbled, realizing I'd said too much.

"So that's how you're acquainted with Mark," he answered, glad to be away from my first question.

At that moment I realized my question was impolite. His world belonged in history books, it was a world kept alive by the knowledge of a few, Portugal's grand masters, a small number of high school riders, and the only horses in the world still capable of carrying out the concentrated movements of the battlefield … the few remaining pure bred Iberian horses with the finest blood lines.

Briefly, he touched my hand, placed his velvet top hat back on and walked away towards the long track that led through the square and then to the salon… disappearing probably forever from my life.

Later that night I thought of the words of Nuno:

'My aim is to allow the horse to work under the rider without tension, to allow the horse to carry out all movements with physical brilliance and mental calm, as though he is free. Any constraint or force reduces the energy he is willing to give to the rider, until one day it is there no more... '

7 Granada

'Last night, mum and I watched people dancing Sevillanas in the old town. Seville's a wonderful city and it always finds something to celebrate. Everyone seems to be preparing for the Easter celebrations, a time when the city opens its doors to the first of Andalucia's spring festivals. Pepe tells me that in the horse parade you can still see Baroque style dressage and horses. Here, the old techniques have never been completely replaced by modern styles, and never will be in this corner of Europe. Even though one part of me would love to stay for Easter, I find I'm over-ruled by my dreams. This morning I awoke with a longing to leave the foreignness of Spain and return to my farm on Yorkshire's moors. No matter how enchanting Seville may be, I yearn to hear the moorland birds and be with Geoff and the horses. My beloved horses ... how I miss them.'

Pepe called the flat today, he said: "Would you like a drive up to Granada, say tomorrow?"

"There's nothing I'd like better ... but tomorrows my last day."

"Then I meet you at ten a.m. at the junction of Callé Betis and Plaza de Cuba. Bring your Mum."

Following breakfast at Manolos we strolled to the plaza, where Pepe sat waiting. "Hope you don't mind the land rover," he said apologetically.

"I don't mind! In Yorkshire land rovers are the vehicles of choice."

"Then we follow in the footsteps of Ganador..."

"Sounds wonderful, I never knew Ganador had visited Granada."

"When Ganador reached the age of one year, I entered him in the Baroque horse championships. The Alhambra Palace and the old Spanish horse are what fairy tales are made of."

After half an hour on steep winding roads, we entered a different world. The flatness of Seville had gone; here I'm in a paradise of natural beauty where every tree and shrub grows in abundance and where lines of tall old Cyprus trees dominate the entrance to Granada's foothills.

From this point on, I'm surrounded by spectacular spring flowers that look to go on and on forever, with a back-drop of sparkling snow capped mountains that tower above Granada, amidst the bluest sky I have ever seen.

Just before the entrance to the province of Granada, Pepe pulled off the road and silenced the engine.

"Here you must listen," he said. For a few minutes I listened hard, but could hear nothing except quiet. Then, I heard a high pitched humming sound which seemed to emanate from below the ground.

"I can hear music!"

"Only when you hear the singing of the water, can you hear the song of the mountain birds. They sing in unison with the water… or so the legend tells us."

"The sound is like the humming of a harp…high pitched and crystal clear!"

"You can hear the sound of music from the melting snow. Lovely isn't it? The melting snow and ice flow through water channels that lay hidden under stone slabs. Look!"

On peeping through a crack in a stone slab I saw and heard the singing of the waters surging down from the mountains.

As we drove higher the icy water tinkled and sometimes it sang like a nightingale. Water spilled from everything, from every beautiful possibility, and every type of vessel had a different tune.

"Everything is in keeping with ancient Muslim art," said Pepe. "The palace is a fairytale castle…it's what dreams are made of, legends too. Here, every room, fountain, ruin or stone has some legend or story to tell … of centuries before."

We had lunch at Pepe's flamenco bar in the old town below the Alhambra and here he told me the story of Ganador's journey to Granada. "When Ganador became a yearling I boxed him up to Granada for the championships of the Baroque horse. And it was here that a quiet day in the countryside turned into a disaster!

Following the competitions a parade was held. The horses were gathered together in the Plaza Nueva, a square that stands immediately at the foot of the Alhambra, and the spectacle looked to stretch on forever. There were carriages and pairs, mares, yearlings, and high school riders in ornate saddles and jewel encrusted bridles. At the back, came the stallions, Spain's heritage of remaining pure lines. A band led the way playing flamenco, with a group of acrobats dressed in white to go with the horses.

All the noise and excitement proved too much for Ganador, wrenching the lead rein out of his groom's hands he bolted past the line of the procession and galloped away up the Carrera and into the hillside that shelters the Alhambra. I can see him now, flying into the distance, his winners sash flapping in the wind." Pepe smiled to himself as though reliving Ganador's exploits. "At the top of the road he turned down a track with lush green grass. He was in no hurry!"

"What happened then?"

"The whole parade turned into pandemonium. When the stallions saw Ganador's departing figure galloping up the road, all hell broke loose. They went wild; rearing and screaming out stallion calls. And then the driving horses joined in the chaos, and a carriage and pair flew down the Carrera, totally out of control...until a wheel struck a rock and the carriage overturned."

"And was anyone injured?"

"The driver had a nasty fall, but thankfully the ladies in the carriage only suffered shock."

"How did you capture Ganador? It must have been difficult surrounded by open countryside."

"Following him in the land rover I walked down the track where he grazed. I knew I could catch him if I managed to keep calm. So I half stood, half crouched near to where he grazed, and waited for him to come to me."

"Why could you not approach him?"

"If I had approached him there was a risk he would disappear down the track which opened into the foothills of the mountains ... perhaps never to be seen again. If I turned my back he would follow me, sooner or later. As I stood there, my eyes fell upon a wooden cross; it was very old and bore the names of a King and a horse. And then I realized I was looking at 'the cross from the legend of the King and the caballo.'

"I love legends..."

"Granada, the Generalife and the surrounding mountains are full of legends; every inch has a story to tell. And this story from old Spanish folklore has always been my favorite." And without saying a word, I waited for him to start...

"Long, long ago, there lived a Moorish King. He lived in a castle that stood on the cliff top above the track where Ganador grazed. The King always left his good Spanish horse saddled overnight, as being a warrior he knew the value of a quick escape. At four a.m. the King stood at his window, surveying the Alhambra and surrounding forest. Suddenly, though the openings between the trees, the King saw a long line of mounted horsemen, each carrying a lantern and moving up the winding track that led to his castle. The leader of the warriors was Queen Isabella of Spain; she was dressed in a suit of chain armor and wore a crown. Isabella had come with her army, to take the Kingdom of Granada back into Spanish hands, after ten years of war.

Knowing his fate if he stayed, the King hurried down to the stables. There, he leapt on his horse and galloped to the rocky lip of the cliff face. At the edge of the sheer drop, he laughed out loud to the invading army and urged his good horse on...and the hoof mark imprinted on the stone that lies buried beneath the old cross, is where a Moorish King and a good Spanish horse, met their death.

The story goes on to tell of how the King left a horde of treasure in a cave under his castle, and how the sounds of pick-axes and shovels can still be heard on nights when the moon is full."

"What a sad story..."

"But the story tells of the bravery of the Spanish horse, and no horse could be too brave or too proud. When the Moors invaded the Peninsular they found the Spanish Christians horses to be better than their own, and much more numerous. So much so, that after the Moors landed on Gibraltar with fewer than one hundred horses, they were able to convert infantry to cavalry following the first battle."

"What was the most important quality a battle horse could have?"

"Pride and bravery were the most desirable qualities. A horse could not be too arrogant. After that, the traits held in high esteem were agility, beauty and a high intelligence... a horse that could out-think his master and save his life on the battlefield."

"Ganador's proud," I said. "When I ride him out, his steps become so high he appears to hover, as if he's trotting the air and not the ground."

"He is displaying his master and showing his nobility. This is what he was bred for... Classical riding and the Spanish horse cannot be thought of separately, the art of dressage at its most advanced level was developed to copy the natural movements of the Spanish horse."

"That's quite a legacy."

"Like vintage champagne he was, and the only proper mount for King's and Emperor's..."

"The enchanted city of Granada," said Pepe thoughtfully. "In my library are many books telling of the myths and folklore behind the countryside of the Iberian Peninsula. Legends are numerous from this period, all conspiring to promote the Iberian horse as a mystical creature, with more than animal intelligence..."

"When did the Spanish horse reach his final form? What I really mean to say is at what point can I think of these horses as the forefathers of Ganador?"

"With the Moors, according to history books," he said without hesitation. "The Moors put the Iberian horse centuries ahead of any other breed. What the Moors brought to Spain was an almost religious attitude to horses and horse breeding. The Arabs created a picture of the battle horse that travelled the World…"

"What is your own opinion of when the Spanish horse reached its best?"

"With the Romans," he said definitely. Under the Romans he was bigger and more statuesque. I think the second cross with the Berber weakened him… but that's only my opinion, others disagree."

After our tour of Granada, we drove up to the Gypsy caves of Sacromonte. The hillside's a honeycomb of caves which look down over Granada; it's like a small town. As I gazed down over the city, views of the Alhambra were breathtaking. The sight of the roof tops of the old town glowing in the sunset was nothing short of magical.

Pepe told me that in parts of Spain living in a cave is not unusual and never has been.

"Can anyone live in a cave?" I asked. "Are they free?"

"The caves used to be free and I can remember the day when the caves were lived in by Gypsies. But then the Gypsies moved away because they were promised better housing."

"You mean the council moved the Gypsies into flats?" asked Mum suspiciously. "I can just imagine a place like this advertized as holiday homes."

"Now the caves are sold as studios or holiday homes with a handful of Gypsy families living in the lower caves to run the flamenco bars."

Doorways to the caves were buried all over the hillside, some with house fronts so they gave the appearance of bungalows, and some in the floor. Pepe's cave was at the very top of the hill, close to the Benedictine monastery and well away from tourists. On entering his cave I felt surprised at how large the cave-rooms were, far larger than the rooms in Mum's flat.

"But where's the kitchen?" I asked. "I've often wondered how smoke gets out."

"Since most caves do not possess chimneys, the kitchens are inside the doorways. Everything has to be very simple in a cave."

As dusk fell, I heard the sounds of flamenco echoing through the structure of the rock. The acoustics were strange but also very beautiful. I wanted the music to go on and on, to pierce the silence of the caves ... and I thought of the legend of a Moorish princess who was imprisoned in a cavern in the middle of a mountain, and how she used the power of music to enchant everyone around her.

The downstairs part of Pepe's cave had the appearance of a great cavern inside the mountain, its walls shone silver with moisture and the floor sparkled with imaginary diamonds. As I gazed at the enormous cave, Pepe told me yet another legend...

*

"Close to the Alhambra and deep underground is a large cavern where hundreds of the finest Spanish combat horses stood in line with their masters, armed with lances and jeweled swords they waited, ready for the field of battle."

"But I can't imagine horses living in caves."

"Better than being out in the open...There were hundreds of horses and warriors coming back to rest or going out to fight in the wars of Granada, and elsewhere. What better place to rest and keep out of sight than a cavern, and a cavern with a fresh water supply?"

"But surely Boabdil, his court and army were exiled in 1492? I've seen paintings of the King handing the keys of Granada over to Queen Isabella."

"Or so it is believed," said Pepe. "But in legend there are no answers...just stories. The legend goes on to tell us that all who took part in the final struggle for Granada were shut up in the caverns by the power of enchantment.

"So Granada is the chosen Caliphate?"

"Apparently so..."

"According to my brother, Spain will eventually be taken over by Russia ... not Allah."

"Maybe your brothers correct ... But the legend tells us a different story. Who knows what the future holds?"

"It seems to me that Granada is still under Muslim influence."

"And it always will be, it's a place steeped in myth and legend from centuries before," answered Pepe.

As Pepe drove back to the flat I formed a mental picture to take home. Strangely, my very last impression of Granada and Sevilla was not an image of delightful buildings or fairy tale castles; it was a sound, the sound of dancing water.

In the still of the night fountains murmured as clear as silver cymbals, around every important building there echoed the resonance of running water, under stone slabs deep underground … only to move on and then reappear as streams or rivers in Sevilla's parks…there to begin its journey once more.

Just before we said goodbye, Pepe said:

"So you can hear the singing of the water?"

"And I can hear the song of the mountain bird! Today's been wonderful; I will never forget your kindness."

"Sometimes, a return to the past can be an opening towards the future…"

*

Al Andaluz 1395

'No animal in the world brings man such benefits and pleasure as the Spanish horse. Because of his noble and proud spirit, it never shuns danger. It fights bravely and rejoices in the success, and sorrows at the misfortunes of its master.

8 The Dream

Just before ten a.m. mum drove me to the airport. I always experienced a terrible sadness when I left mum, it was like a light going out and it never became any better. As she turned away she said, 'give my love to Ganador and Geoff, and see you in summer!'

As the Boeing leveled off I listened to the Captains voice and unfastened my seat belt. Settling back in my window seat I gazed at shafts of light burning holes in the white vapor we call cloud. For something to do, I took pen and paper out of the abyss of my bag and listed the many stories of Ganador. As I wrote the first words I felt a surge of excitement, flowed into over drive, and in less than half an hour had written two pages on the subject of Ganador's adventures. From the first word, I allowed Ganador to take over. I tried to see the stories through his eyes…and only then, through the eyes of those around him. After all; Ganador's exciting life had been far more exciting than most history books.

From the first time I saw him, in a scrap yard owned by Gypsies, to his training on the Yorkshire moors, and then back to his origins in Seville, I wove together his amazing story, a magical journey that had introduced me to Portugal's grand masters, swept me through the end of a civil war and brought me together with a race of people I'd never known before… the Romanies. By digging deep into the past of his forefathers, I'd discovered fascinating legends and stories about his ancestors, the battle horse of King's. The horse that founded classical equitation… for it must never be forgotten that the art of dressage at its most advanced level was developed to copy the natural movements and abilities of the Spanish horse, natural movements that had created a new art form...the art of classical equitation. There must be people like myself who longed to find the source of equitation, longed to find a prototype of the ancient battle horse. And sitting there above the clouds I wrote the first line of chapter one:

'It was a freezing cold morning in early March when I saw the advert that changed my life...'

On this short holiday I had glimpsed a little of Ganador's past, discovered parts of his life that would otherwise have remained a mystery. I thought of all that Pepe had told me, of the stories, legends and history that belonged to his ancestors. And I reflected on the help and advice given to me by Fernando, my mentor, my learned professor.

At that moment I made a vow to tell others what I had learned through the medium of Ganador ... and in so doing allow others to share his amazing life. And hopefully the courage of his ancestors would shine through my words and stories, telling readers of the enormous sacrifice given by both man and horse.

'Come down to earth,' said my inner voice, you're returning home to Geoff, the horses and Ganador. Just keep in mind the important words of Pepe ... 'the rest of his story will be written by you...'

As I thought about my holiday a world of memories flooded back. And then I must have fallen asleep, for I had a dream, a dream so real I entered another world...

'Suddenly I returned to the magical city of Jerez de la fronterra...I was on holiday with Mum and Dad and the year was nineteen seventy three. We sat in a shaded Moroccan style café set amongst tall jacaranda trees and all around the air was alive with cheerful cadenzas from hundreds of tinkling bells.

"Listen," said Mum, she held up her finger the way she always did. "Listen to the sound of bells on the driving horses." Mum loved Andalucia, she said it had a charm all of its own.

And then Dad broke the spell as he always did, he wasn't a dreamer like Mum and me; he was a practical man always conscious of arrangements and time.

"What about strolling through the park to see the jousting

tournament? Air conditioning and horses Norma, and we just have time."

At four p.m. we walked through the lovely grounds of Parque Gonzalez Fontoria to the competition hall. As we entered the lights gradually dimmed and any chatter died away.

And then I saw him... he came galloping into the arena, his silken mane was heavy in gold braid, thick wild curls almost touching the ground. Every line of his exquisite bone structure shouted of fine breeding and history. This was surely the horse as painted by the great masters, whose exploits in combat had known no equal. This horse was the Battle Horse of King's, and he was awesome.

When he galloped his whinnies thrilled me, for he sang from his heart, melodious, bell like cries. The cries were not the whinnies of a normal horse; they were nothing less than rapture, of pure joy.

"His melody is hauntingly beautiful," whispered Mum. "It's nothing like a whinny." Mum seemed hypnotized by this creature. "Look at his eyes, brilliant and staring. Watch how he considers every detail."

I watched light dance and shimmer through his silken mane, casting a magical silver pool around him.

"He soars through the air...just like a bird," said Dad. "His movements are almost of the air and not the ground; as if at any moment he might spread his wings and fly..."

Dad handed the program to me. At the bottom of the page were the following words:

Bred for bravery and beauty

Pure Spanish Baroque line Cartuhano

'It should be plainly seen that the Spanish horse enjoys carrying its rider and being watched by spectators.'

1677 ... Riding Manual

As I read these words, I knew I watched history repeating itself, right here before my eyes. I also knew there must be admirers of the Spanish combat horse who still bred horses from these ancient blood-lines. And I made a wish ... that one day I might own such a horse...'

Abruptly my lovely dream slipped away, I tried to waken up but felt trapped in this other world. Hesitantly, I looked at my surroundings… the tournament had gone away and I was completely alone. I glimpsed images of waterways, smelled the sweet perfume of oranges, the perfume of Seville.

'There was a narrow pathway between tall palm trees. Huge leaves hung heavy and still in the night air. The only sound was the sound of dancing water, from hundreds of fountains, streams, and watercourses … the song of Seville's old town.

At the point where the trees ended, there was a bridge over the Rio Guadalquivir. I think it was the Puente de la Cartuha. At the other side of the bridge, I stepped onto a moorland track. I recognized the path, knew it well. Yet I never questioned how the land beneath my feet had changed from a Spanish continent to an English island.

The path ran into the middle of the north Yorkshire moors, and was located close to my farm. I was familiar with every rise and fall in the rutted track, the ancient stone wall that lay in ruins, the bramble bush on the right but not the left.

After walking up the track, which surprisingly felt flat and easy under my feet, I came upon a Victorian mansion house. It stood in the center of spacious grounds. There were no walls, just a wooden gate. I opened the gate to walk down its short drive, and saw the most wonderful sight. Golden light glowed and flickered across the driveway, like a mirage in the desert. As I entered the light, I immediately knew the true meaning of happiness … an endless stream of eternal peace. Nothing mattered anymore except a longing to stay in this other world.

Outside the house, a group of men sat on forms arranged in a circle, just passing the time of day. Leaning forwards, the men watched carefully, as if playing a board game or listening to the end of a story.

My curiosity encouraged me to walk towards the men, and there I saw the strangest sight. The men were gathered around a chess board, an enchanted chess board. All the pieces moved by their own volition, soldiers marched across the board, horses whinnied and tossed their heads, castles threw down their draw-bridge. When the King moved I heard the sound of a trumpet, whilst the Queen played a silver harp...The sounds echoed hauntingly in the silence, quiet, yet clear as a mountain stream.

All of a sudden the chess pieces halted, but not before I saw the King lift his arm as if to point. Following the direction of the King's arm I watched a young man stand up as though his name was called and walk peacefully towards the house. He looked happy; how could he be otherwise? There was no need to feel afraid. Not here. Was this a place where words were unnecessary? Where communication was through gesture, thought, or something unknown to me? And were these men being guided to their final destination?

Sitting on the form closest to the house I saw Dad. I raised my hand and waved, but he didn't see me. I thought of calling out, but my lips were sealed. Suddenly, I knew I had no access to this other world. But it didn't worry me ... Dad looked so very happy.

So I walked towards the marble pillared entryway. Within the hallway I looked at thousands of tiny brass plaques adorning either side. Each had a number. Written under the number was a name. In the bottom corner, I found my own name ... the number was twenty six. Strangely, I did not feel surprised. Neither was I afraid.

Entering the house, I followed the numbers. I had to find out where my presence rested. On the first floor, I found a door numbered 'twenty six.' I opened the door and walked in. For what seemed to be an unclear time, I stood completely still, staring at an empty space. So beautiful and dreamlike was this space, that it defied description in mere words. From the window, I watched people young and old entering or departing. But I never saw a child. I never saw the moor. Around this community, the air shimmered gold. But the sun was not the sun I knew, it was different to the hazy, gentle sun of the moors ... neither was it the searing sun of Spain. Here, there was no need for any sun. All around the house and grounds, light glowed. The kind of light I'd never known before ... the radiance of time without end.

Unexpectedly, a hand touched my shoulder. I looked round and saw two women. They wore sari's, their long hair was braided in plaits. The woman standing beside me took my arm. Gently but firmly, the women led me away from paradise.

'It's not time yet,' said the first woman.

'You have to go back,' insisted the second.

'But I want to stay,' I pleaded. 'This is where I belong.'

'The living cannot see the dead,' the voices sang together. And the women led me out of the house and down the drive. Past strangers speaking silent words, away from where I wanted to stay … but I saw only blurred faces.

The two women walked with me, down the track that ended at the graveyard, but stopped before their feet touched the road. They watched sympathetically, from their non-existent side as I entered the world of the living. With a heavy heart I turned to say goodbye. The women were soon lost in a cloud of mist, but I remember a voice speaking from far away.

'There are many houses… One day you will return.'

Before I walked away, I stared up at a sign. A shimmering light surrounded it. The mist had almost hidden its existence. The name on the sign was 'Sharma.'

Circling the graveyard I walked down the track to the farm. Before me lay the pasture, sloping gently downwards to the gorge, behind the gorge, stood the stark hills I loved to gaze towards. For a moment I stood very still just taking in the beauty of the scene, watching hills climbing into a sea of clouds. And then I saw Ganador, he sang out a whinny before vanishing into the clouds. Beyond this, there was no farm, no stables, just empty fields…'

"I can't find the farm!" I cried out…'

Suddenly I awoke in a cold sweat, wondering how close to the unknown I'd really been. An elderly lady in the next seat touched my arm, 'Are you alright? I think you must have been having a nightmare.'

"No, it wasn't a nightmare," I almost shouted. "I want to remember it to the end of time as the most beautiful dream I've ever had."

"I interpret dreams," the woman said. She obviously wanted to share my dream. So I told her the story. As I spoke, she closed her eyes and concentrated. When my story came to an end, she said: "Your dream was a vision … A passing image, crying out to be seen, to be heard."

"But where was the farm and why did Ganador fly into the clouds?"

"The farm had vanished from your eyes. One day you will live elsewhere. And one day, Ganador's spirit will be free."

"Tell me," I asked, "the meaning of 'Sharma?' I've never heard of the word."

"Sharma, is a word from an ancient tongue, but still used even today. It means, joy, peace, and happiness…"

Toby Jug Farm

North Yorkshire Moors

Spring Time 1981

9 Moorland Spring

Toby Jug Farm, North Yorkshire Moors, Spring Time 1981

Diary April 14 1981

'It's wonderful to be home... Today is the fourteenth day of April and the weathers bleak and freezing cold, but despite the arctic feel, I know today is the first day of early spring. I recognize this time of year not by sunshine or warmer air, but by the cries of mountain birds as they soar down to the gorge.'

The mountain hawks swooped low over the farm yard, causing me to drop the washing. For a moment I thought one of the enormous birds was about to land on my head, so I held out my arm and whistled, but it flew away. The return of the mountain birds is always a special time. I love watching them swoop low over the chimney pots, screaming cries of delight as they soar down to the meadow where the hares run free and crystal clear water sparkles with sprinklings of ice from the melting snow.

"Can't stand this killing spree," Shelly shouted angrily as she came running into the kitchen. "Those poor hares sound exactly like human babies."

The air was alive with terrified pleas of young hares as two Birds of Prey soared low over the meadow, hovering effortlessly, as they scanned the ground. Suddenly, the powerful birds pounced, like flashes of lightening, seizing and carrying the screaming prey into the air, clutching scissor like with sharp talons, before gliding down to the gorge.

"But they're only babies," she said angrily, turning the radio up to full blast. Shelly looked close to tears…She hated the savagery of nature.

"It's a grim scene – but it's finished now, the screams seem to have stopped…Can't alter nature." She turned the radio off and walked to the windows overlooking the valley, as if nothing had happened.

"Red Kite's," she said knowingly. "Beautiful aren't they… and an endangered species. I should be honored they called in for lunch. Sorry for going on Norma."

"Hurts me too…"

"Whose birthday have I missed?" She gazed enquiringly at the single card on the Welsh dresser "Is it Ganador's birthday today? And I didn't know…"

"It's his first anniversary at Toby Jug Farm. Fancy eating out?"

There are certain things that just have to be celebrated, and Ganador's first anniversary was such a one. Voting for an evening of jubilation we abandoned our thermals, dressed in our finery, cleaned out the land rover and headed into the next valley, where our gentle, caring Hebden Bridge doctor had opened up shop as a restaurateur. Dinner was delicious, cooked by his latest girl friend, who just happened to be a professional chef.

"I wonder if running a restaurant gives better returns than practicing medicine."

"Probably similar," said Geoff as he looked at the bill.

"As long as the food's good I don't care."

"Fancy the pub?" asked Geoff, probably thinking of the cheaper prices.

And we drove along the moorland road to the Shepherd, a seventeenth century Inn where every stone, flag and cobble held secrets of times long ago. The Inn was an important place to listen to local hearsay and meet local farmers, who met either to gossip, amuse passing tourists or tell fascinating stories. In the comfort of the saloon bar strangers quickly became friends, even though it was advisable to stand at a safe distance from the fragrance of local sheep farmers… otherwise known as 'hill billies.'

Living high on the moors was like existing in a dream world, everything was different to the world of the lowlands. Even the local farmers looked similar to Victorian beggars with mud spattered boots, army trench coats and baling band belts.

Nothing much happened near the clouds except the sigh of the wind and evenings in the local Inn, nothing except the weather, which in winter came wrapped in a package named violent.

The hamlet of Moonraker Heights could be said to be an insular location. Not many people stayed after their first winter. Dreams of idyllic country life were quickly shattered when they found the moor was at war with whatever weather the moor chose to hurl at it, or when they discovered the family car had to be changed for a land rover in order to drive in snow or on ice, followed by the shock of finding the roof needed renewing... if only to keep dry. And then the golden days of summer came along, magical days, when the perfume of the moor and the song of the mountain birds caused some people to forget the bad times and want to stay.

*

On entering the dimly lit bar, we sidled over to sit close to the fire. 'Let's try to stay unseen,' whispered Shelly. 'So we can listen to gossip in peace.'

"There's no gossip tonight," replied Geoff. "Herbert's brought his television in."

"Television should be banned from places of cultural interest..."

"Don't be silly," said Geoff. "The poor man must need a little relief. Imagine seeing the same faces night after night."

"What do you mean seeing?" questioned Shelly. "The place is almost in darkness?"

Lights were kept low in the Shepherd, at either side of the fireplace subdued wall lights whispered faint rays of gloomy light on stone flags. The local Inn was kept exactly as it once had been - any sign of comfort came from the open fire. It didn't require modern day trappings. Anything less than three hundred years of age would spoil its special aura, destroy what it once stood for... an important hostelry where history oozed from every stone flag and wooden beam, a place where highway men and stagecoach passengers had once of a day stood side by side.

Tonight, Carlton sat in his special seat at the top end of the bar. He called this spot his watchtower; it faced the door, the entryway to the Inns barn-disco. The barn was used by local hippies, most of who lived on top of the moor because of its cheap living and lack of nosy neighbors.

I watched Carlton shift in his seat, he looked away from the television as if he was trying to ignore its presence. Carefully he checked his watch, hoping the intrusive voice might go away.

"Norma!" said Geoff. "Look at the screen... Carlton's been up to something."

Now, the voice boomed out, it filled every air wave in the room. Herbert adjusted the volume to his satisfaction and a still silence descended over the bar as the interviewer read out an advert from a newspaper:

'For sale ... Caravan plots on Yorkshire's enchanting moors. Ideal for caravans or long term investment. The country plots are adjacent to good walking country and premium Yorkshire Inns. Prices start at only £10,000 per plot.'

"That's your farm Carlton," said Herbert. "It's the one near Lancashire boundary."

"I've done them all a favor, that's what I've done," replied Carlton. "Tha can't find countryside more beautiful than yon farm."

"Tha can't sell Yorkshire's moors Lad," replied Herbert. "It's not thine to sell."

The announcer on the screen appeared fascinated by the idea of selling the moors, and said he would love to live close to a premium Yorkshire Inn.

'North Yorkshire is one of the most beautiful parts of England, a county with charming old towns and stunning scenery. And it's also a location with its very own language, a mixture of old English, Yorkshire dialect and traces of what some experts think may be a Celtic tongue.'

"Silly bugger," said Carlton to the man on the screen.

"How many plots did tha sell?" asked Bert.

"Best speak to them in charge of access approval at town hall." Carlton glared righteously, Bert went quiet. He knew there was no department of access approval...not on Yorkshire's moors...unless Carlton had put someone in that position, very recently.

"What 'av tha been doing Lad?" said Zachariah quietly.

Carlton made a show of lighting his pipe, always a slow workmanlike process. "This lot," he said brandishing his arm at the television, "are trying to make me sound like some no good money grabber."

"Let's listen to him not you," said Bert sharply. Turning on his heel Carlton walked away from his reserved seat and sat by the fire with Geoff.

"What's been going on Carlton?" asked Geoff.

"Fixing folks up with a piece of paradise, that's what."

"Caravans need hard standing not bog Lad," said the gentle voice of Zachariah. Carlton and Zak were friends, although the two men were opposites in looks, speech and thoughts, there was a certain comfort that one got from the other, an acceptance of each other's flaws, that made the moorland saying 'what I do for thee ... thee can do for me,' immediately understood.

As we left the Inn the action on Bert's T.V. suddenly changed to drama, with scenes of towing trucks pulling a caravan out of bog. Only the back wheels had sunk, the weather had been kind recently. Rain had only fallen for six hours each day, not the usual twelve.

The distraught caravan owner stood talking to a woman holding a microphone, 'this is my receipt,' he said angrily, pulling a neatly folded envelope from his pocket...'

"Yet another of Carlton's G.R.Q. schemes," said Shelly as we crept out of the Inn.

"What does that mean?"

"Get rich quick of course. Just imagine selling the moors, what a brain wave!"

Laughing, we drove down the track towards home. The moon shone metallic silver on the frost covered pebbles and in the distance Ganador sang out a soft yet ringing whinny.

"He's missed you," said Shelly.

"And I've missed him. Seville has nothing on this...It's wonderful to be home."

As Shelly went round with extra hay, Ganador's timeless eyes looked straight into mine. Resting my cheek against his velvety nose I felt his magic, his energy. A power I never quite understood.

And I thought of Mum's words:

'You either fall in love with a horse, or you walk away ... and if you fall in love, prepare to have your heart broken...'

10 'Gypsies On The Moor…'

Diary April 20 1981

'Today the color purple casts a shimmering haze on the pasture beneath the hills. From the farm window I see a stream of lavender light lazily making its way up the footpath towards the stables. I never can resist gazing at light and cloud flooding into the valley. The allure of endless pictures passing before my eyes… images I will always remember.'

That afternoon I rode Ganador over the moor to Zak's farm. As far as I could see the moor was covered with gorse, reeds and heather, except in the shelter of stone walls where rushes grew, mixed with the odd clump of blackberry bushes and thyme. Not everyone's idea of beauty, but I loved watching the vibrant rhythm of the moor, the phenomenon of light and cloud endlessly passing over its wilderness, the magnetism of the moors endless detail and colors changing through the seasons. The moor may be bleak and abandoned but it has its own energy … it's a power I can feel all around me.

Zak's farm stood in a clearing, surrounded by large rocks and dry stone walls. He kept a few sheep which were usually gathered around the farm house door awaiting his presence. Zak knew each of his sheep by name, a fact that always amazed me.

For a time he talked of Carlton's latest exploit, "Lad says he's a steward o' moor and it be nowt but bog without him. I tried to warn him, I said, 'tha can't sell grazing rights Lad', but he carried on like he always does."

Zak sat on a wooden box in the doorway; his sheep looked

expectantly towards him as if awaiting instructions. Today he wore a long duffle coat and army boots, his military medals hung from a picture hook on the white painted walls inside the porch.

"Too cold for wearing uniform," he said. "I saw this 'ere coat on Todmorden market, it's as good as new." He pulled up the collar of his new purchase and tightened its belt. "It does as an extra blanket on bed at night…"

"A little present for you, it's from Seville," I handed him a hand painted fan; it showed an image of the Alhambra palace with a background of snow capped summits.

"Wait till Carlton sees this…" Opening the fan he held it up to the light to examine the image within. "Bloody lovely, it'll go on wall."

"Help keep you cool in summer."

"Tell me about Spain," he said wonderingly.

So I told him how I'd met up with Mark and Pepe, 'the Romanies who once owned Ganador.'

"Talking o' Gypsies," Zak said awkwardly, "there's a letter 'ere, addressed to you it is."

"What's a letter for me doing here?"

"Gypsy lad rode o'er with it. Not much more than a boy he was. Nice Lad as Gypsies go…sat himself on a bucket and sharpened all scythes for free." My heart jumped with excitement thinking of the letter.

"Maybe it's from Marks mother, the Gypsy woman who taught Ganador to sip tea," I said. The letter must have traveled down 'Romany way,' the unseen pathway of the traveling people that passes from hand to hand, from family to family, until arriving at its destination.

"Granddad," boy said, "do you know of a Spanish oss, name of Ganador?"

"That I do," I told him. "Know it well."

"When you give this letter to Ganador's owner you'll have money and luck for life. That's what he promised." Zak smiled thinking of the Gypsies prophesy, he pulled a greasy envelope out of his shirt pocket and placed it in my hand.

"Before tha rides away, av a question Lass…Would tha like to see Gypsies tonight? Lad says they be passing o'er moor."

"I'd love to Zak, but don't tell Geoff. You know what he thinks about Gypsies."

"I promise Lass… but Geoff doesn't know what he's missing."

"Geoff thinks like Carlton on the subject of Gypsies."

"Thav said it all there; Carlton can't abide them."

On returning home I saw to Ganador's needs, turned off the stable lights and sat under the single bulb in the tack room. With a swift tear, I opened the greasy envelope:

'Dear Norma and Geoff,

Having Ganador back at the yard for Mark's wedding to Evita made us all very happy and we thank you for your kindness. We loved that horse, we've missed him so we have, missed him more than you could ever imagine. Perhaps you've wondered what Ganador was doing with Gypsies? His last owner wanted rid of him, and ordered him sold at Appleby fair, so that no-one would know of his whereabouts. So the men gave Roland a run for his money and took Ganador up to Cumbria, but with no intention of selling him, not at a horse fair. They just went through the motions of selling, giving him a price tag that no Gypsy could afford. Adams may be a hard man, but he promised me he would never sell Ganador to any Gypsy dealer. You see, we fell in love with the horse, and even Adams said he was a King's horse. Adams also said that all the Gypsy dealers he knew would sell the horse for meat rather than be made to look a fool of, and Ganador's an expert in bringing a man down so he is.

But Ganador made two good things happen. At Appleby, he introduced Mark to his future wife, Evita. And he found you, someone who understood him, who would give him a chance. Memories of the day you brought him back for the wedding will always be with me.

May good fortune be yours……Mother Adams.

For a long minute I sat staring at the letter re-living the night of Mark's wedding. Just thinking of the Gypsy family brought back memories I wanted to lock away in some crevice of my mind. As I placed the letter in the bottom drawer I felt something small in a corner of the envelope. Shaking whatever it was onto the desk, I watched a tiny medallion fall out. The design was of a seven peaked crown over a script written S...the same insignia as that of Ganador's brand...

*

At seven I left the farm, feigning a visit to a violinist friend in Burnley.

"Have to collect some music," I said as convincingly as possible.

"Better drive back round Todmorden, could be a busy night for townies," shouted Geoff from the stables.

"Will do..."

With a sigh of relief I drove towards Zak's farm, pulling off the moorland road and parking behind farm buildings, well out of sight of passing motorists. Finding Zak waiting in his land rover I jumped in. He drove westwards, towards Lancashire, past the shooting club and out into the country side.

"Lad said to drive up this track o'er Mereclough way."

There was a track, hidden by rushes, covered by undergrowth which led to the outer moor. To the right I saw a packhorse stone, a large stone with a rounded top, a centuries old signpost for horses and carts leading out to mines or hamlets. Now the only sign of life was the distant echo of gunfire from the range.

Without any warning the track ended in a clearing close to a stream, "Better get out 'ere." Zak whispered. Walking further up the track we saw spiraling smoke from a fire. "Lad said wait 'ere."

In the distance there were five large touring caravans and just one peddler's wagon, the same wagon I'd seen on the inner moor. Lights glowed from windows, warm welcoming lights of the non electric variety.

Between each home, horse's grazed the rough moorland vegetation as though it were the sweetest clover. We stood behind a stone wall listening to the faint sounds of a flamenco guitar, not knowing what to do next.

"Listen," he whispered, "listen hard Lass... it's the sound of Gypsy music out on moor. It makes me want to be a traveler!"

There were two guitars and a flute playing now, the sound of the music echoed across the moor, it was wild and free. A cry of freedom from the race of the humble, that would join with the song of the wind and be as one with nature. And then it stopped...leaving a hum of voices and the distant bleating of sheep.

Out of nowhere, a Gypsy boy appeared. The boy shook hands with Zak and bowed to me. 'Welcome,' he said, 'follow me.' Leading the way across half a field he stopped at the entrance to the first caravan. 'Careful,' he said, some steep steps led to a door. 'It's open,' and I stepped inside. The room was full of Gypsy women of all ages, there were only two men and the boy.

'Ganador's new owner,' the boy said. The moment the women heard Ganador's name, the unseen barrier that exists between Gypsies and other races seemed to disappear.

"Any friend of Ganador is a friend of ours," said more than one voice, and I was ushered to a seat in the heart of the room.

"So you know Ganador?" I asked.

"We're devoted to his breed," said my neighbor. She touched my arm and greeted me with a hug. By now I felt only friendliness and warmth.

"Thank you for bringing the letter." I said, trying to take in all the faces in the room. Everyone smiled, except for a young woman who eyed me suspiciously. "It must have been difficult finding me out on the moors."

"We searched for Ganador, we knew we'd find him in the end," said the boy quietly.

"I saw you at the Romany wedding," said the young woman. "Ganador made a beautiful holy horse. Evita needed him."

"So you know Evita?"

"I'm acquainted with her family, we travel through France and occasionally we visit Andalucia." The younger woman had a strong foreign accent, short blonde hair and was dressed in expensive clothes, with lots of gold. "Sometimes we join up with the El Rocio pilgrimage as it travels along the Atlantic shores."

Suddenly an older woman with weather beaten skin and a lovely smile took over the conversation. "I'm friends with Marks mother … she adored Ganador. Mother Adams taught Ganador to drink tea from a china cup… with milk and two sugars." All the women nodded in agreement.

"She begged me to continue with his treat…"

"And did you keep the promise?" the girl with the blonde hair asked.

"Yes I kept the promise," I replied. "Ganador has tea every morning, and he sips his tea just like a gentleman." The instant my words were spoken I knew I'd fallen into her trap.

"Ganador's a King," the girl said harshly. She pounced on my inaccuracy, "He can't be expected to drink like a common horse." She smiled, but not at me, and I knew that what I'd said had let Ganador down in some way.

As if to relieve the tension, the woman sitting next to me started to speak, "The stallion was a good friend to Mark's Mother."

"Pity we can't say the same for Adams, can we?" said the older woman. "Put the fear of God into Adams did Ganador!" The women laughed as if remembering Adams secret fear of the stallion.

"You must be very special," said the young woman, "to have been given the chance of Ganador…there are not many Ganador's in today's world."

"I write on the breed and study the Iberian horse."

"And you've just returned from Sevilla?"

"Well yes I have," I pretended not to be surprised at the girls knowledge, the traveling world was small, and news moved quickly. "Pepe and Mark told me things about the Spanish horse I never could have imagined. I'm interested in anything that relates to the origins of the Iberian breed."

"The mystery of the sacred horse," said my neighbor.

"Tell me…" I asked, taking advantage of the lull in the conversation, "what would have happened to Ganador if I hadn't come along?"

"Pepe would have taken him to France, most likely the

Camargue area. There are still a few horse farms near the marshes where they don't ask questions."

"You mean he would have disappeared…"

"No-one would ever know," the girl said with a certainty far beyond her years. "Romanies from all over the world know of the Spanish horse. We understand that the old Spanish blood lines are superior in every way."

"He is the perfect horse in every way," said the older woman.

After drinking tea with the women, it was time to go. Thanking them for their hospitality, we were again escorted back to the track.

"What did you make of that?" I asked Zak when safely inside the land rover.

"Gypsies have it all up 'ere," he said tapping his head. "If I were in your shoes, there'd be extra security on Lads stable door…"

11 Showtime

Diary April 30, 1981.

'Spring is show time, a time of year when we travel the horses out to competitions. Geoff's a far better competitor than me, he loves being in the ring and meeting people. I'm the opposite, and going out to strange places never becomes any better than nerve wracking, and sometimes I start worrying weeks before the event. The thing is, boxing horses out to shows has to be done. Horses have to be socialized, have to get over their fear of strange noises and bustle. I imagine the same applies to me... but try as I may, I never get over mine.'

Over one full year has now passed since the arrival of Ganador, almost four hundred days, filled mostly with delight. So much has happened during the past year... Fernando, my Portuguese trainer has taught me the principles of classical equitation; spelled out knowledge that is not widely known or understood. He's become my lifelong friend and mentor, in the training methods still used by the remaining Portuguese grand masters; he's also my learned professor in the history of the Spanish horse.

My world has opened up; I think and train differently with the knowledge that everything may be possible, even if only a little.

The best thing to come out of all this, is that Geoff and I have realized that all physically sound, correctly trained horses are capable of learning that little bit extra, 'the icing on the cake,' as Geoff puts it.

And with this in mind, his jumping horse Donovan became his next target in training after the manner of Ganador...

"Hunter classes here we come, we may or may not win a rosette but there are other compensations!" Geoff laughed suspiciously; he was keeping something to himself. Shelly looked down at the carpet her face flushed with embarrassment.

"Like what?" I enquired patiently. But he made no reply. He didn't need to. He looked at Shelly and joined her in admiring the carpet, a fact which caused me to feel worried about any secret plans - without him having to say a word. "Surely you wouldn't show me up... Not in Cheshire, surrounded by all those hunting people, and not in the show ring. You really can't be serious..."

"Wait and see," was his guarded reply.

*

Two weeks later, we accompanied Donovan and Ganador to what was to be their first ever show hunter competition, held in the much warmer county of Cheshire. The sight of our seventeen hands high, heavyweight Irish 'hunter' performing Spanish walk around the show ring created a definite stir, especially amongst the more conservative show hunter followers.

Surprisingly, a smile appeared on the rock like face of the judge who seemed eager to share the secrets of this new pace.

'How does one give the aids to obtain his expressive walk?' the judge queried. The stern judge then rode Donovan with Geoff walking at his side with the intention of finding out just how to obtain such a walk.

"What a talented fellow," he said. "Does he hunt?"

"One of the best out of Ireland," replied Geoff, "and hard as nails."

Shelly shook with laughter, having to pretend to blow her nose. 'Sod the Judge,' she whispered. 'Don's having a whale of a time ... I think my boys look incredible!'

When the judge saw Ganador, he looked puzzled. "And what breed is this horse?" he asked Geoff.

"Spanish," replied Geoff.

"Never knew they hunted in Spain."

"The terrains difficult, but you'll never find a more genuine horse than this lad."

"Foreign hunting horses in Cheshire…never thought I'd see the day."

Amidst the hue and cry of hunting horns and barking of hounds the judge climbed aboard Ganador. The fun began when he took up the reins. Immediately the stallion felt his stronger than average contact on the reins, he decided to walk backwards out of the arena and through the crowd of spectators standing outside the ring. On spotting a steward advancing towards him, so as to lead him back into the ring, Ganador twirled a pirouette and cantered to the middle of the show field.

Fortunately, the judge stayed in the saddle throughout Ganador's escapade, though he appeared somewhat dazed by his experience. When safely back in the ring, the now white faced judge carefully applied his leg aid, which caused Ganador to perform piaffe … not an ordinary piaffe, but one of the most splendid I had ever witnessed.

By now, the judge knew that Ganador had taken over. He also knew he was completely at the stallion's mercy. The crowd gasped in astonishment as the aimed for walk across the arena turned into a waltz style sequence of pirouettes.

'Astonishing,' said a voice from nearby. 'Never knew the old man could ride like this.'

"Hear that?" said Shelly. "He thinks the movements are directed by the judge!"

To finish, the judge lowered his hands, probably to dismount as quickly as possible. But the signal had only one meaning to Ganador, that of passage. And with high hovering strides, he passaged all the way around the show ring…

Following our picnic lunch, eaten outside the horse box, we proudly drove off the show field with two large rosettes hanging inside the windscreen for all to see. Leaving the landscape of Cheshire's flat green fields, we drove through the mill towns of Lancashire where rows of identical terraced houses seemed to go on forever. Gradually the scenery changed to villages which formed the periphery of the moor and quant hamlets with pubs and restaurants.

Mist was rising in the valley when we entered the steep winding road to the high moor and ribbons of steam rose from the peat earth.

"Lovely isn't it?" Shelly said dreamily. Suddenly she pointed to a large truck on the opposite side of the moorland road. "Look," she said. "Gypsies are off somewhere. Just imagine spending one's life traveling about..."

I watched the departing vehicles disappear in a blur of mist. "How many caravans passed?"

"Three," she said confidently. "I counted three caravans and one peddler's wagon. Carlton says they've been parked out on the moor." Without knowing why, I felt the first pangs of worry. Surely there were five caravans out on the moor... which left two unaccounted for.

*

The following morning, my worry took on a form I never knew existed...blind panic. It began when Geoff rushed back into the house.

"Ganador's not in his box," he shouted into the kitchen. The moment I heard his words my heart seemed to lurch. This was the worry I'd locked out of my mind. Throwing on a coat I ran flat out down to the stables, only to find Geoff staring at the lock from Ganador's stable door. "Broken," he said grimly. "The field gate's open too."

"It's not possible," I screamed. "I remember shutting it." Shelly looked distraught and started crying.

"Calm down," said Geoff. "Everybody calm down..."

The instant he'd spoken, I heard hoof beats. Not hard and metallic like the sound on a road, but soft, like distant thunder as if on earth. "He must be on the pasture, maybe he's grazing with Fred." And we set off down the footpath, carrying a torch, head collar and rope.

In the damp mist of early morning I followed Geoff down the

footpath and into the gorge. Swirling clouds of fog rose from the river in the base of the chasm, making visibility unreal. And then I heard Geoff's voice. "Found him, he's down by the river." On climbing down a rocky incline, I found Geoff holding a broken fencing post. "Look at this," he pointed to a gap in the fencing. "Three posts gone and the wire's pinned back," he said. "Must have refused to go through the opening, most likely started rearing and scared them off."

"Sure the Gypsies didn't pay him a visit complete with mares?"

"Don't be silly..." he said. "Bit of a mystery that's all."

"It's where he's been in the night I'm worried about... Gypsies are camped on the moor."

"Why would they come over here?"

"Ganador, that's why. And more money when they sell a mare at Appleby fair, especially when it's in foal to a Spanish stallion." Geoff chose not to speak and I knew he would never refer to the incident again.

Without saying another word, he caught up Ganador and led him back to his stable, with Fred following in his tracks.

As I walked back to the stables I thought about my secret meeting with the Gypsies and Zak's words: 'if I were in your shoes, there'd be extra security on Lads stable door...' I remembered the haunting sounds of music out on the moors and what appeared to be their genuine friendliness in bringing the letter.

Then my common sense took over and I heard the Gypsies sing-song voices saying, 'any friend of Ganador is a friend of ours.' Why had I believed their words...?

12 A Chance to live...

Perhaps a lack of foresight caused me to overlook Geoff's secret training of a third horse, perhaps I should have been suspicious when the lights from the indoor school burned half an hour longer than was usual. But being a firm believer in openness, lack of secrecy and doing the right thing I believed the excuses as carried by Shelly "Geoff rakes the school floor now at seven. Easier than having to rake it in the mornings," she said before carrying on cooking her healthy evening meal. I knew I had nothing to worry about regarding Frederick, my dressage horse, my very own personnel possession.

"Just leave my horse out of any training plans" I had sternly told Geoff some weeks earlier "I don't want any icing on the cake with Fred"

"Doesn't need any," he replied, "he's sweet enough." And he nodded in agreement.

There were two reasons why Fred meant so much to me, why I acted as his guardian. The first was that I had taken him in, given him a home when no one wanted him. A worm infested, ugly, skewbald colored colt, living wild on the open moors. Abandoned by passing travelling people on their way to Appleby Fair and already feared by walkers for his tendencies towards biting and kicking. To meander down any footpath close to where Fred grazed was an open invitation to be attacked.

"A danger to the public." the local police said. "Threw a hiker over a wall last week, picked him up by his rucksack. If the rogue can't be caught, a marksman will get him."

Dual of the White Arms sketch by Sue Triggs

Ganador Piaffe, Geoff up

Fred and Norma, early morning exercise

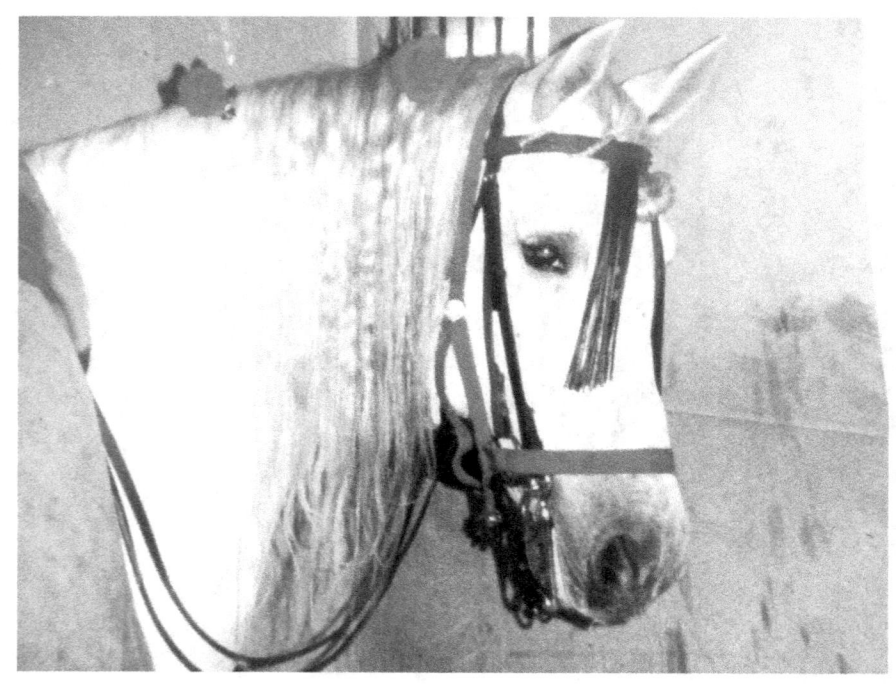

Ganador, before the display

Campanero in Passage, Samantha Grimes up

Free at Last

And so it was that Fred the mixed up colt came to reside at Toby Jug Farm. The second reason was his accident, one of the worst days of my life, a day I would always remember in vivid detail. The accident happened more than three years ago but the horror of that day had never faded. Every word said and image seen would forever be with me.

It was the first Monday in May, the year was nineteen seventy eight, the time almost twelve noon when the accident happened. All of a sudden I heard a deafening roar, it sounded like low thunder falling out of the sky. Simultaneously there was a piercingly loud bang. I looked up and saw a fighter jet streaking over the stables, so low he seemed to skim the chimney pots. We dived for cover, Geoff swore and I screamed. The plane was so near the ground that I could easily see its windows and pilot. There seemed to be a large card with identification numbers in the side window of the plane and for some reason I felt surprised about this fact. I stood and watched the jet disappear into the distance as it followed the contour of the pasture down into the valley before it rose vertically into the clouds, vanishing amongst mist covered hills.

For perhaps two horrifying seconds the noise reverberated all over the valley. Donovan reacted to the shock by furiously kicking his stable door. In Fred's box I heard the unmistakable sound of crunching stone, then silence.

"Pity he can't reach the bloody pilot," shouted Geoff angrily.

"Just imagine breaking the sound barrier when flying low over farms, must be a damn idiot"

There were only two horses in the stables that day, Fred who waited to be shod, and Donovan, all the others were out grazing on the bottom meadow. Donovan seemed to direct his whinny across the yard towards Fred, then gave his door another hefty kick... but around Fred's loose box there was an empty stillness, certainly not his usual 'what's happening out there' head nodding trick, which drove me to distraction.

Running over to his stable I looked over the door and called his name. To my horror, Fred stood at the back of his loose box trembling in pain, attempting to balance on three legs, his right fore held in the air unmistakably broken, dangling like a rag from above the fetlock joint. Geoff and I stared in disbelief, only seconds ago, moments that seemed like hours, we had laughed watching him dreaming, dead to the world, sound asleep.

"Obviously dreaming of something exciting look at the way his legs are moving!"

"It's a galloping dream," I said. "He's racing down to the bottom meadow to play with the hares!" At that moment I never imagined that a split second of terror was about to shatter his life.

In the three years he'd been with us Fred had become part of the family, a good friend, a little horse with a big sense of humor who could easily unlatch all loose box doors and loved to stand with his nose poked inside the farm house window. He still had temper tantrums, his hate towards hikers had never diminished, but we all loved him. The ugly foal was now grown into a smart good looking horse showing the beginnings of exceptional paces and jumping ability.

When David the vet arrived, I will always remember his every word, so clear and God like. And more than anything I will never forget my feeling of total despair.

"Broken at this spot and here too," he said pointing to the all revealing radiograph. "Cartilage shattered too, and there's no blood supply to cartilage. I'm sorry Norma, but there is absolutely no chance of complete recovery." He paused to clear his throat; I already knew the words he would say, "I'll do it now if you wish..." He spoke in a soft kind voice, the voice of a man who had travelled this path many times before.

But I knew what 'do it' referred to, it really meant 'kill,' put him down, out of his misery, asleep, they were all kinder ways of saying 'finish him off.' I wanted to scream, to waken up from this wretched nightmare. Geoff brought me back to reality, he said, "Norma what do you want to do?" Now there was silence, nobody spoke or moved. The men waited to hear my reply. This was my decision; mine alone.

For a long moment, I stopped thinking...my emotions got in the way. Maybe it was a gut reaction or some kind of hunch, but suddenly, I knew exactly what I wanted to do.

"That won't be necessary," I sobbed hysterically as I stroked the nose of my hobbling horse.

"I'm giving him a chance," I whispered. "A chance to live…" David saw my tear filled eyes, heard my choked voice and frowned. He stared towards Geoff, but he just nodded too. So David went to his car, pulled open the door and carried back his first aid case. He wanted to say, 'you will never ride him again,' but he stopped himself and set about putting a light plaster cast on the break, which perhaps for five incredulous seconds enabled him to stand on four legs.

"Beyond this, there is nothing I can do. Complete rest and one injection night and morning for a week," he spoke to Geoff now, probably thinking I was in shock.

"No chance of recovery Norma, certainly not for riding purposes. No blood supply to cartilage." David smiled kindly saying, "Ring me when you need me… just for a chat," before walking over to his old Volvo and driving away up the track.

Geoff gazed at the plaster cast and frowned. Taking out his knife he sliced it straight down the middle, from top to bottom.

"Are you mad?" I said incredulously.

"I'm taking it off," he said. "He needs rest, and this cast will stop him from getting down."

"What about support?" I screamed. "His break needs holding together."

"I'm bandaging the area; have to be redone every four hours though. And I'm changing his box to somewhere quiet; don't want him moving about…not too much." Looking at me he said, "What about moving him into the old sitting room?" Geoff considered his plan carefully for a few moments, and then nodded "Well I think it's a good idea…"

"I suppose it is…" I replied, this time without any hesitation. I remember wondering why I held Fred's lead rope so tightly when he could only hobble. "Is he changing boxes now?"

"No time like the present," said Geoff as he climbed into the hay loft.

*

The stable block held a fascinating history of times past, having once been the cottages of farm workers. Each loose box had once been lived in, and had splendid stone fireplaces, bricked up now but still ornate, original flagged stone floors and a door step to the front. The largest old cottage possessed three loose boxes, front living kitchen with mullioned windows looking over the valley, weaving room and back sitting room.

The old sitting room stood to the rear of the stables with views of the moors. It was roomy, quiet and had the advantage of not looking into the yard, ideally suited for a restful unknown period of habitation. For six months this was to be Fred's home, his diet high in calcium and minerals, his walking or hobbling confined to the limits of the floor area.

At the end of five months, Fred stopped hobbling and began taking delicate steps around his sitting room stable. With daily fomentations of hot and cold, plus careful bandaging, his fetlock began to feel cool to the touch, the puffy swelling almost gone.

After a while, Geoff shod him with higher heeled shoes plus shock absorbing pads. "Helps cushion stress on the fetlock joints," he said, "ready for his big day when he takes his first walk outside."

I expected the transition from loose box captive to fresh air and freedom to bring out all or some of Fred's worst behavior, rears, bucks, charging away, perhaps even towing me with him. After all he had spent six months in the horse equivalent of solitary confinement, sitting room or not, it was still prison even if it did have country views. In fact none of this happened; he walked sedately at my side, once round the farm yard stopping only to nibble some grass. He then continued with this exemplary behavior by proudly walking back to his sitting room box. At the doorway he briefly halted and called out a few 'hello I'm here' whinnies to his friends...

For me, the tension was unbearable and time after time I found it necessary to check his support bandage, just to make sure his leg was still in one piece. After a further three months of walking in hand I just had to admit that I was being over protective towards Fred.

The day was fast approaching when a few gentle strides of trot were on the cards, and that day became imminent when Geoff said, "Trot him down the long side of the school or I refuse to shoe him. No excuses; just do it. How do I know he's sound if he never trots?" And so I trotted him for a few strides with Geoff loudly applauding. "Tomorrow morning," he said. "I insist on riding Fred, just to see how he feels."

My nerves were like jelly the following morning, just waiting for the worst to happen. But the worst did not happen, and Fred trotted happily for short periods in and amongst his walking.

"When a break mends, it should be stronger than ever - he needs exercise now." Geoff spoke over his shoulder as he gaily trotted past where I stood, and to my amazement Fred was still sound after one week of light exercise, a fact which never failed to embarrass David our vet.

"A miracle," he said in his scientific voice, his face crimson red.

"A miracle he didn't end up as horse meat David," Geoff replied in his most sarcastic voice.

"One chance in a million you know, his break was not straightforward." David said hesitantly, hating the humiliation.

"If they are all destroyed it has to be!" Geoff started to laugh… and thankfully David laughed too.

When Fred did not show any signs of lameness for several weeks, my confidence in his soundness slowly returned and the irrational fears of him falling apart gradually crept away. Just as everything seemed to be progressing smoothly, fate struck another blow and Fred went lame behind. Not in one hind leg, but in both…

"Luxation of the patella" said David "Could be an inherited weakness, possibly brought on by his extended rest"

"What would you do David?" As I said these words I felt completely drained. All the fight had gone out of me. So I put the decision making into David's hands.

"Operate" he said without hesitation "No good for anything as he is" The following morning David operated on both hind legs, cutting the ligament responsible for upward fixation of the patella's. "Prognosis is good" he said smiling warmly "With a slight possibility of arthritis later. But if I put him on this medication now, he should be fine" At the gate David wound his window down, handing me the bill. There was no charge, just a line of zeros and a message which said 'all things are possible.'

After four weeks of steady walking exercise … we started over again and this time I could only hope there would be no looking back.

'All things are possible.'

13. Ganador's Friend Fred

Toby Jug Farm May 14 1981

'Today is exactly one year and two months after Ganador's arrival... it's also the time that Fred and I have tiptoed into medium level dressage. I feel so proud of him; he has certainly beaten the odds. David the vet was so right when he said that all things are possible. I think Fred has taught everyone a lesson, and teaching a vet a lesson must be near impossible. There's also one other good thing, Fred has become Ganador's best friend! Ganador and Fred are what Geoff calls soul mates; they graze on the same paddock and spend hours standing close. The strange thing is that both horses have the exact same character traits, they frighten the living daylights out of hikers, hate rucksacks, throw shopping bags over footpath walls and think nothing of jumping back and forth over a five barred gate. Geoff always says the same thing: 'what can you expect when they both served time with Gypsies? Has to be a cause somewhere in their past...'

Following his long imprisonment, operation, walking marathon, high heeled shoes and special diet ... Fred was back, even his canter felt exactly the same as before, perhaps even better. Once again he galloped down to the bottom meadow and raced along with the hares. Fred was at last enjoying life. Gone were the weeks of pain when he stood in a corner of his box staring at a wall and refusing to move, weeks when the most important part of any day was to minimize his pain.

And so I shook myself out of my guardian angel role and entered him in the spring dressage event to be held in the grounds of

89

Haydock Park racecourse and daringly entered the FEI Medium 32. I filled in the entry form and with my heart thumping with excitement drove the six miles to the nearest post box. That evening, after I told Geoff about the forthcoming event I noticed a worried expression cross his face.

"Can't wrap him in cotton wool forever," I said. "I thought you of all people would be pleased."

"Of course I'm pleased," he almost shouted. "I fought a running battle to keep your horse alive. Or had you forgotten?"

"No I'd not forgotten. And why are you being so defensive?" "It's just that I was thinking of taking Ganador over to Haydock Park."

"Taking Ganador to Haydock Park, for the dressage?" I said in astonishment. "You must be joking."

"Not to enter any competitions of course…just to ride him on the showground. It's known as getting experience. Let's take both horses… they seem fond of each. We could hire two temporary boxes on the field."

"No problem at all," I replied, knowing my calm day out with Fred had just vanished.

But Geoff continued to look gloomy, his face told me that something was wrong, Geoff was one of those rare people who find it impossible to disguise how they feel; his reactions were there for all to see.

"You have the look of a worried man," I said warningly. And then I played my ace card by pretending to know all about his little secret.

"Why not do the decent thing and tell me why you are not pleased?" I asked. "After all… Shelly knows everything." Michelle could not argue as she was in the school walking Fred.

Geoff sighed and stared somewhere above my head, all with a total absence of eye contact, a character trait I found highly suspicious.

"Follow me," Geoff shrugged his shoulders, he could not care less. "As you already know," he said cagily. "There won't be any surprise."

And so I followed him down to the indoor school only to come face to face with Shelly exercising Fred. What surprised me was the way she held the reins; she was working Fred on the short rein. Something I had never taught her.

"Can't remember teaching you short rein work…"

She glanced furtively towards Geoff and said, "Geoff gave me a lesson."

"Gave you a lesson with my horse when I was in Seville…"

"Well I'm off…" she said, staring at the floor for support. "I have so much work to catch up on. See you later!" she sang out, swiftly escaping out of the door.

Now it was Geoff's turn to hold the reins, walking at Fred's shoulder down the long side, he said, 'Watch this… you will be amazed."

And to my amazement and horror, my horse went into a stunning piaffe. Not any average low to the floor shuffle, but high stepping and rhythmical. My role as trainer had just been demolished by Geoff, and I felt annoyed, humiliated even.

"How long has 'this' been going on for?" The criticism in my question was starkly obvious. I tried desperately to look and sound unimpressed "Fred is my horse and you never asked my permission." I allowed myself to yield to my inner fury; my cool had become hot, boiling in fact. "So this is what you call a surprise? Teaching my horse circus tricks behind closed doors, a horse recently escaped from the threat of becoming dog food…" Geoff interrupted my tirade by irritating me even more.

"He found piaffe easy, he's what you call talented, and thus far he's my star pupil. But look at this!"

My face remained stony to rocklike as he signaled Fred into passage. The passage was excellent, though I could never admit it, not at this moment anyway and contained lofty steps with definite suspension. I hated the way Fred was enjoying this new work, his ears pricked, his body totally relaxed, and without any sign of stress. I really wanted to continue feeling angry, but astonishment and pride kept pushing my anger to one side. Then, I remembered the dressage test.

"I'll have to cancel the dressage test now, all because of your fooling about. How can he understand my aids clearly now he knows some more? We will be the laughing stock of the show. I can just see him in passage rather than collected trot or messing about in piaffe rather than halt." How could he do this with the test only six weeks away? "You have gone too far this time or are you planning a tour with Kit and the tiger woman?"

Geoff looked surprised by my worries and began to search for what he considered a soothing, reassuring reply. He was thinking, 'anything to stop the nagging,' it was written all over his face.

"I'm sorry I didn't ask your permission. I thought you would be pleased. Why not allow me to ride him in the damn test; if I have your permission of course."

"No problem at all" I replied "You have my permission to ride him; I just hope you are up to him."

Geoff was at a loss for words and started drawing boredom patterns in the sand with his schooling whip. I began to soften, to see the humor in the situation, Fred obviously enjoyed his new role as a high school horse, he looked so very happy. It didn't really matter about dressage test thirty two; I would let Geoff worry about evasions and confusions.

"I must admit he is talented" I heard myself say already dreaming of riding Fred in effortless passage.

Later that same day, with Geoff walking at my side, I rode Fred in piaffe then passage and felt his incredible power and ability.

"This is like heaven" I purred "what a brilliant little horse" I could not help but smile, as a result of which poor Geoff sighed with relief.

"Do not teach him Spanish Walk," I begged, already suspecting this request was too late. My theory or best guess was indeed correct and Fred's Spanish Walk exceeded the height and stretch of that of Ganador, it was nothing short of spectacular.

14 The Dressage Competition

May 22 1981

When the big day arrived Geoff held true to his promise, and insisted on riding Fred. The weather was heavenly, not too warm but with a sky of brilliant blue and fluffy feather light clouds, a perfect spring day. Positioned in the middle of the park was a small area decked out as a fair ground and in close proximity were two exercise arenas, surrounded by large crowds of spectators.

After unloading, Geoff took the two horses down to the stables, riding Ganador and leading Fred at the same time. Shelly carried picnic hampers and I wheeled the large tack box. The stables were sited at the far end of the park near the forest and were shaded by a setting of oak trees. After filling Ganador's hay net, Fred was given his final polish and tacked up. Everything was perfect.

I felt very proud as I followed my team down to the exercise arenas. Fred looked magnificent with his tiny plaits and braided tail and I knew Shelly had been hard at work since dawn.

To begin, Geoff worked on Fred's paces, his walk trot and canter and Shelly glowed with pride and satisfaction.

Quite abruptly, the remarks of a horsey faced man who was standing next to her turned our happy day upside down.

"Never imagined anyone would dare bring a colored horse here," the man shouted into Shelly's ear as he wagged his finger towards Fred. "It reminds me of a gypsy horse, common as mud," he spoke in a derisive manner laughing loudly at his own comments.

If looks could kill Shelly and I would be serving life sentences for murder, as Fred was our pride and joy. Shelly grew at least six inches taller before turning towards the man and staring him square in the eyes.

"Shelly," I hissed. "Please don't punch the guy. He's just not worth it. We could get banned from the showground."

And then Shelly spoke rather than punched "I believe he is a Gypsy horse sir," she stared into the man's eyes with hatred. "This man has a problem Norma… ignore him." She shouted the words with lethal loathing, and the man turned and walked away.

What happened next was a series of events that defied all my expectations. Geoff started to display Fred's high school work on the practice arena, which included Spanish Walk, piaffe and passage. In the background, music from the roundabout drifted over, the tune was teddy bears picnic and everyone clapped in time to the music. I stood rooted to the spot with shock but Shelly seemed amused.

"This is what riding is all about Norma, enjoyment! Can you hear the nice people applauding?" She sighed with pride "All my work has not been in vain," she said quite seriously. If I could have chosen to be airlifted back to the quiet emptiness of the moors, or even spirited away from all this hustle and bustle I would have gladly taken that option.

The spectators however loved every minute, probably thinking this was a show put on for their enjoyment.

"You do realize they think Geoff's giving some sort of a display?" said Shelly proudly.

By now I felt shaken to the very core. "This is a British Horse Society dressage event … not a circus."

I could not believe what I was seeing but suddenly the loudspeaker stopped all the fun by announcing that test thirty two would begin in thirty minutes time down at the quieter end of the showground.

Feeling humiliated and sick with nerves I followed in Fred's hoof prints, walking very slowly to what felt to be my death. I was terrified.

"What if he enters in Spanish walk?" Shelly laughed at my

fears. She had not a care in the world.

"So what?" she said humming the strains of teddy bears picnic "The spectators would love it, adore that little bit of showmanship. Personally, I am enjoying every minute. Try to calm down Norma. I have always held the view that dressage tests prove nothing. In my opinion it is arty farty nonsense." She meant every word, and clutched the bag of grooming equipment even harder.

Unexpectedly she dug me in the ribs with her elbow "Norma," she whispered, "we are being followed, pretend not to look" But I did look and to my horror saw the same group of spectators who previously enjoyed Fred's high school display on the practice arena.

"Geoff," I shouted. "Your fans are behind you. Perhaps they think you are giving another circus display?" But he didn't hear, it was too late, and my words were left hanging in the air.

"My numbers wanted down in the collecting ring," Geoff's voice rang out, and without a trace of nerves he cantered Fred away.

When we arrived at the competition arena, there was nothing to do except take our places and wait.

"I wish I'd stayed at home," I said to Shelly as I watched competitor number one finishing his test. "I can't stand this tension."

"Everything's in the hands of the God's now," she said. "Try to relax Norma." I stared down at the Olympic sized arena and realized how right she was. All was too late...

As the moment of Geoff's entry drew near, every noise became silenced, every eye seemed to focus on Fred, the only colored horse on the field... and then the bell rang. Hardly breathing I watched horse and rider canter down the centre line. His halt was just right; it was straight, balanced and submissive.

"Come on Geoff!" shouted Shelly. Her voice seemed to trigger Geoff's supporters into action, and the crowd who had followed us down from the practice arena, simultaneously gave a round of applause.

"Please Shelly, this is dressage not football," I weakly pointed out. Though I need not have worried, for we were to see both horse and rider at their very best. Geoff rode Fred through the movements of this difficult test proving beyond any doubt how completely Fred understood the aids for walk, trot, canter, shoulder in, half pass and just about everything a horse can possibly do… without including one step of any movement not written on the test sheet.

Out of thirty two entries Fred was brought in third, and yet again the applause and cheers resembled the noise of a football match.

"Not bad for a badly bred Gypsy horse is it Norma?" Shelly was laughing with pure delight "I'm glad you stopped me punching old horse face, because with any luck he may have seen Fred doing his stuff."

At that moment the world was good, I felt heady with joy and full of parental pride. My once abandoned ugly foal with a once broken leg had achieved more than I ever dared hope for. Not in my wildest dreams did I imagine he would impress the judges, not at this level.

"Time for Ganador's outing Geoff," said Shelly adjusting Fred's extremely large rosette "You must be exhausted after all that effort." She proudly walked alongside Fred, down the path leading to the stables.

"Stay with the hampers and don't move," shouted Geoff over his shoulder. After what seemed like an hour, but was only ten minutes, Shelly returned. "Fred's back in his comfy box with hay, and Ganador should be with us shortly. He's enjoying his day out and he isn't nervous at all!"

At that moment I heard Ganador's shrill whinnies coming our way, and then I saw him entering the exercise arena in a high, suspended passage. He looked dazzlingly beautiful, and for a long minute everyone stopped and stared at this strange, magnificent creature.

"Geoff said he's too excited to walk," said Shelly sighing blissfully. "Doesn't Ganador look divine? And just listen to the applause," she said proudly. "I'm so excited Norma!"

And then 'he' appeared, our enemy, the man we called horse face. I could see him standing by the ringside.

"Nothing but a circus horse," he shouted angrily.

On hearing his voice we both stiffened, waiting for more of his cruel remarks to bite, as we knew they would.

"Don't take the bait Shelly," I warned.

"I'm surprised the organizers let him on the field," the man yelled. Shelly could not take any more... and the inevitable happened, she turned on him.

"People like you, are...are...," she stammered, "animal racists." She screamed her words venomously across the exercise arena. "Ganador's the most beautiful horse on this field...." Her uproar went unheard, because of the start up of the roundabout, to the tune of teddy bears picnic.

"He's gone Shelly, given up." We watched the man walking away...until he was out of sight.

"Thank goodness he's gone," she said breathing a sigh of relief. "He almost spoiled my day, and days don't come any better than this one. Well ridden Geoff!" Suddenly she was happy and beamed a blissful smile "Today has been a heavenly day, a day I will never forget. What sensible judges!"

That night, the evening mist was down over the moor as Geoff drew into the narrow road which led to Toby Jug Farm. The whole character and feel of the surrounding countryside had now changed. The greenness of Haydock Park had gone away. Here there was only wilderness and silence. When the horsebox pulled into the yard Ganador's whinnies pierced the silence of the night, echoing mysteriously inside the horsebox.

"Turn the lights on damn it!" Geoff shouted into the mist as the engine shuddered to a halt. "I can't see a thing."

"Sorry Geoff," replied a sleepy voice. "I must have fallen asleep."

"But you are not asleep now;" Shelly shouted from her side of the horsebox, "turn the lights on immediately." And suddenly the stable yard became bathed in light. "That boy thinks of two things, eating and sleeping," she said disapprovingly as she climbed down from the cab.

"Kettles on plus I've conjured up sandwiches," said Kit trying his best to appear industrious. "How did it go?" he spoke to Shelly now, Geoff and I were only the ornaments.

"It went heavenly!" she purred as she lowered the ramp. "Third in medium and a special award, I don't know what it's for though..."

"I do," said Geoff, "best turned out and most promising Northern dressage horse." Geoff always knew how to halt a conversation. "Tell him later," he said leading Fred down the ramp and across the yard.

Shelly peered into each loose box with her torch "Just checking how long you slept for!" she said to Kit.

"But a good day was had by all?" he persisted, avoiding her question.

"The best day of my life..." she sighed glowing even brighter than the yard lights.

Yorkshire Moors, Summer 1981

15 When Blackbird's Sing All Day ...

Diary May 31 1981.

For eight long months I'd dreamed of a day like today, a time when winter just dissolved away into the riches of spring. A new world had started to emerge, a world of color and softness. The meadow and hills were fast becoming a multihued tapestry of tiny moorland flowers, and sweet smelling cotton grasses. This was the time when birdsong filled the air, when blackbirds sang all day, when the call of a cuckoo broke the silence of early dawn calling hauntingly from the gorge. But most of all during the month of May was the scent, nothing was real except the scent, it lingered everywhere, behind every doorway, on every breath of wind, earthy and sensuous ... the perfume of the moors.

"What a beautiful morning," Shelly groomed Donovan in the washing yard, she still wore the satisfied smile of success, she had worn it since the show. "Life can't get any better, I feel so happy."

"You're reliving yesterday, the five minutes of fame. Was all the effort worthwhile?"

"Worth every second, even the five a.m. start." She led Don back to his box, heaved the last bale of straw into the feed room, and finished by checking the stable doors.

"Bolted and secure," she said. "Bye boys, see you later." Shelly always talked to the horses, the odd thing was, they listened and sometimes seemed to understand her every word. We strolled to the edge of the yard, climbed over the stile, and made our way down the footpath to the gorge. At the highest point we sat on rocks gazing at the hills...Shelly said she could always rely on the hills being there, unlike some people.

"Just look," she called from her position next to a half dead tree, "all the snows gone."

"Last night was warmer than usual." Every trace of snow had melted away leaving the verdant green of new grass. I never tired of looking at the hills, of watching colors change throughout the seasons, I never would.

As we gazed at the view, ribbons of silver mist clouds flooded into the valley, hovering above the lowland towns of Todmorden and Hebden Bridge. When the gathering of mist reached the level of the gorge ... a sea of snow white clouds ascended, kind of grew out of the mist, spreading out across the valley, forming a carpet of clouds, beneath the farm, beneath my feet. They were endless. Each one was equal in size and symmetry; each one had a twirl on top, just like ice-cream cones. For a time the rest of the world ceased to exist, we both stood in silence gazing at the beauty of nature.

It was then I felt the concussion of hoof beats on the earth, and heard the blowing of a horse.

"Here's Geoff," I whispered, trying not to spoil this special moment. Geoff rode Donovan bareback, he'd come down to see the miracle of the clouds, to get a front seat.

Geoff broke the silence first-

"Low layer cloud, cumulus variety. Only happens when the fog rises, and ..." Shelly completed his sentence.

"And the air pressure is just right, but I don't want to know why. Look at the tops of the hills climbing out of the clouds ... it could be a painting in a story book. I think it's magic."

"I do too," I said turning to go, "makes me want to ride over the moors, far away from the last inhabited farm..."

Each spring I felt the same longing, I wanted to rediscover the inner moor, a place called 'no man's land' where the wilderness appeared to go on forever and ever, where the land lay wild and unfarmed. After I'd made coffee, I set about finding a partner for the ride. My first target was Geoff,

"Fancy a ride across the moors?"

"No way," he said. "I'm finishing that supporting wall in the end cottage, and this is the last push."

"I'd forgotten…"

"Have to press on when the sun shines - or I'll never finish."

After Geoff I looked at Shelly,

"Too much to do, and I have a driving lesson."

I saved my final plea for Kit,

"Your call Kit," I said hopefully.

"Do I have to go? The last time I set foot out there I lost a shoe to a bog."

And so I saddled up Ganador and set out alone. After a while I came to the entry of the inner moor, a deeply rutted soil track which lay almost hidden behind the old grave yard. Morning sunlight slanted in long thin strips across the path, casting shadows of gold onto the land. Everything was exquisitely beautiful. The track passed a scattering of farms until I came to a place where all civilization had died, to where the land opened up into one huge expanse of wild moorland.

This was the no man's land of the moor, a place where no one lived nor trod its paths, no man, no animal, except the poor sheep who had nowhere else - a place where even the sun was in terminal decline, swallowed up by thick low cloud, so very low I felt I could almost touch them. Any warmth there may once have been had died away, leaving a permanent, penetrating chill. Yet the place held a strange fascination for me and each year I returned to its wilderness, its silence.

When the track climbed over the horizon of the moors, I halted Ganador, for some reason I started to think of Mothers words … What she said as we stood outside the farm for the very first time.

"Shhh…" She placed her index finger across her lips and stood completely still, as if waiting for the last sounds of life to die away. "Listen to the silence of the moors."

I'd never listened to silence before … I didn't know that silence could be so many things, heavy or light, tuneful or frozen. Mum said that in the middle of the moors, it could even be 'immense,' like the final whispers of death. Mum was very dramatic.

"No-one proper would want to live out here."

"What do you mean by proper Mum?"

"Proper people live together in groups. We don't fit into any of the named boxes, into the structure of society, we haven't got a label."

"You mean we are outcasts?"

"In a way ... But is being an outcast such a bad thing?"

"I really don't know. Maybe it is or maybe it isn't."

But what I did know was that Mum adored the moors - she said the stillness helped to recharge her batteries, whatever that meant.

"Helps me think more clearly, be aware of all that's around me, if you know what I mean." I always listened to Mum, even though she made the most curious statements at times. Saying things I didn't identify with, that made no sense... at that moment in time. But a short time afterwards something always happened that helped me understand her every word, as if the meaning had forever been there at the edge of my mind, just waiting to be understood...

At the place where the soil track ended; and the endless trails of dry stone walls were no more, a narrow pathway of sorts lay covered over with peat soil and rushes. Only a few remaining cobble stones still showed the way, they were scarce and set at irregular intervals but just enough to keep Ganador away from the peril of bogs, the unseen scourge of the inner moor.

I was never prepared for the sight that lay ahead, even though I'd seen it many times before. In the distance stood the ruins of a centuries old hamlet, it was surrounded by clear green areas, where no rough moorland vegetation grew. The disguise of verdant green grass was often one of the tell tale signs of bog land, so I gazed at what was left from the pathway, wondering how on earth the stones had been carted to the middle of a bog. Maybe sometime in the long gone past the land had once been fertile? But then I wondered what happened to make it bog?

I could plainly see the shells of four derelict farm houses, on the ground floor were narrow slits for windows. The farms had been built to give the outward appearance of a perfect square... within the center of the square stood the remains of a large barn. Although in ruins, it was plain to see the perfection in configuration of this centuries old hamlet, it was obviously built by persons with more than a modest knowledge of planning, which always set me wondering about what kind of society had once lived in this settlement. Maybe centuries before trees or even forests had grown out here? There may once have been sunlight...

All of a sudden as though at some prearranged time, the low cloud seemed to hang down lower, billowing mist clouds casting a foggy haze over the light of day. The feeling was of winter, damp and cold with the distant sound of a howling wind. I began to shiver, longing to return to the warmth of my less remote farm and disappear from this wilderness.

Turning Ganador towards home I carefully followed the damp shining cobbles by torchlight. The mist moved ahead of me dense and swirling. When I arrived at the place where the paths came together I felt overwhelming relief. Here there was sunlight, warmth, the sounds of birdsong. Ganador screamed a whinny as he stepped out of the last mist cloud ... he knew he was heading home. Compared to what I had just been through my return down the rutted track seemed very low key, there were no sudden mists or bogs to watch out for. The only exciting event to occur was in the form of Zachariah who lived in one of the last inhabited farms, grazing his few sheep on the open moors.

"Av been waiting for thee lass," he called from the wall he seemed to be continually repairing. "Thav bin lucky today tha knows." Zak paused to allow the full implication of his warning to enter my head.

"Tha still be an off comer, don't know dangers." Off comers included those whose residency on the moors fell short of twenty years. "Mighty strange world out there - bogs and gravity does some funny things tha knows." He stepped over the collapsed wall to stroke Ganador and together we walked slowly down the path. He was dressed very smartly. His sheep farmer's rags were hung out on the clothes line taking an airing. Today he wore his old army uniform. The edges of the sleeves and lapels were threadbare, but it was neatly ironed, and he was proud to wear it. He saw me looking at his uniform, and his face lit up. "Dost tha like it Lass? It must be well o'er forty year old and it's as good as new" On Sundays and Mondays he proudly wore his war medals, the history of each I knew well, the place, the time, and the action.

"Take care Lass. And remember sea mist drops down afore this hour, never lifts in winter"

Zak admired Ganador, who started to become difficult. He tried to spin but found the path too narrow for this maneuver so he changed tactics and displayed a few strides of passage "Does Lad want a cup o tea? I don't mind going back and making one" Zak loved to see Ganador sipping tea - he said it made his day. But I had to get home, if only to prevent Shelly from worrying.

"I think Ganador wants to get home quickly Zak."

"Best stay away from t' wilderness, tha could o lost that good oss to a bog." I thanked Zak for his advice. He offered me his hand, and I shook it. The skin of his hand felt just like the rough bark of a tree ...

"Before tha rides off, av got something to say," Zak took his cap off, he held it across his chest, I watched one of his medals lifting in the breeze. "Carlton told me about Lass o'er in valley ... Terrible shame. Lass 'be same age as Elaine was."

I went on my way, shielding my eyes from the low glare of the sun. Why hadn't I remembered dark glasses? They helped if only a little. The intense brightness always seemed more extreme on this pathway; it hurt my eyes with its power.

At the bottom of the track I saw Amber. She stood at her easel sketching the entryway to the moors wilderness, she looked lost in thought. When she noticed me and Ganador walking towards her she waved. Amber wore a beautiful velvet waistcoat the color of emerald green. It was decorated with heaps of sparkling sequins arranged in designs that looked like Egyptian holographs. Her coffee colored skirt fell in folds almost to the ground - she could have been a ghost from long, long ago, waiting for a stagecoach. Amber always looked different she definitely wouldn't fit into any labeled box. Then I realized she was already in one, the label of London hippy, trying so hard to appear dissimilar, but surrounded by people who lived in the same group.

"I love your waistcoat Amber."

"It's Moroccan in design ... Popular on Todmorden market," she paused, and for a moment neither of us spoke. "Ian told me about Abi yesterday."

"Her children don't know yet, they're too young."

"Has she got long?"

"No, I don't think she has ... Maybe a few weeks or months?"

"The authorities refuse to admit the cause was the spring water..."

"The powers that be will never admit the cause was a cocktail of spring water and sheep dip. That's why they rushed a mains water supply up here. We have no evidence... the proof has gone."

"That makes three... two deaths and Abi just waiting."

"And no-one will ever know the truth."

"I'm writing to the press, even though it won't do any good," she said thoughtfully. "And I've written to a science magazine."

"The drug company withdrew the dip last year, or so they say, but it continued to be sold. Can't get anywhere with drug companies."

"Is this the kind of thing that often happens in the countryside?"

"Not often," I had to swallow hard as I spoke. Whenever I lied I had to swallow, it must be some kind of nervous reaction about not being honest. How did I know what poisons were being concocted in some drug companies laboratories... pesticides, herbicides, sheep dips?"

Amber reached out a hand to Ganador,

"Can I touch him?" she asked.

"Of course..." She stood against his shoulder with her arm around his neck, and placed her cheek upon his mane. He gave a soft whinny of contentment.

"I'd love to paint him, together with a background of mist and head stones."

"What will you call it?"

"Battle Horse of Kings, he's to represent the ghost of a battle horse ... Ganador will be a wow on the markets." Amber subsidized Ian's passion for buying and selling things of beauty with her paintings, all her scenes were details taken from the graveyard or the open moors - until now that is.

"Come down anytime, I think Ganador would love to be painted."

Geoff had told me about Abi only last week:

"Wait a minute" he said "I've something to tell you … I've just done the pony's feet, from the farm in the valley," he looked round the room as though searching for words. "You know Abigail, the young woman at the farm... she's got terminal cancer." When he said those two words, I felt incredulous, Abi was living not dying.

"But she's only thirty two … What about the children?"

"Her Mothers living at the farm, tells me she's in no pain."

"So it is the Doctors car I see every morning. That makes three locals in the last few months."

The first local was Tim, the veterinary sales man. I bought wormers and disinfectants from Tim. He used to visit each month. When Tim didn't arrive with my order I rang him.

"Its Tim's wife," a woman's voice said. "He won't be coming again, he's dying."

"I'm terribly sorry…"

"You're not to know. He's only got days, its spread to his throat."

Tim was fifty two. Tim died in February.

Then there was Vince, the new barman at the pub. He went out and bought a new American camper van, Geoff said he wondered where he'd got the money from.

"Why work in a pub when you can spend fifty grand on a van?"

"He must enjoy the banter."

I thought of the night when Vince brought his wife to the pub to help him serve, and I remembered Carlton saying, "Tha could have spent money on a farm... something solid."

"He's always wanted a camper van," said his wife. "He wants to tour Scotland before his numbers up. Lad can put his head down anywhere, anytime in the van. Whenever he's tired, he can have a rest." And still I did not realize.

Vince was forty seven. He died in April. He was on holiday

touring Scotland, somewhere he had always wanted to see…

In all three cases, it seemed as though a terrible mistake in diagnoses had taken place, they all seemed so healthy. Yet all died of similar cancers … in near identical ways.

I never met the man from Black Edge Farm again, or any of his family. Rumor had it that he died in hospital, aged sixty three. After his funeral the house and land were put up for sale, then auctioned. Carlton told me it was sold to a gang of Manchester hippies. The health and whereabouts of the original family from Black Edge Farm remain unknown…

*

As I rode into the stable yard, I watched the sun going down, casting strips of golden shadows across the pasture. The color from the hills formed a sparkling haze over the meadow. Today the color was golden. The light danced and shimmered just like gold dust in the air. Only a reflection from the flowers on the hills but so very beautiful compared to the darkness of 'no man's land.'

The clock struck six when I entered the kitchen; Shelly sat reading whilst Kit watched television.

"Where have you been?" she queried "I was starting to worry."

"No man's land, but the mist came down," for some reason I felt like a naughty child. How could I start to explain how fascinating the remote parts of the moor were in spring?

"Personally, I would never venture onto the moor, and certainly not alone. There are many variations of remoteness, here at home is pleasantly remote, but where you have been is one degree past dangerous." Shelly was so levelheaded and rational. She reminded me of a strict teacher.

All of a sudden there was a voice from the choir at the back of the room and Kit joined in.

"My Gran, warned me never to go out there, she said strange people meet there in Midsummer, sacrificing chickens and worshipping the sun. An evil place she said, full of terrible secrets."

"Your Gran may be right, but the sun isn't co-operating with whatever they may be doing, it's freezing cold out there." After saying this I made a mental note to keep well away from no man's land especially at the time of any Midsummer ritual. Kit went back to watching his cartoon favorites. How cartoons could make anyone happy had always eluded me.

"Turn the television down," Shelly growled a warning across the room to Kit. "And tell me what your Gran knows of 'terrible secrets?' Out with it Kit... you either know or you don't know." She put her hands over her ears and sat with her back to him, which for some reason made him talk all the more.

"My Gran told me that bodies of sacrificial offerings are at the bottom of the bogs," said Kit cheerfully.

"I wonder how Gran knows that... Neither do I believe they worshipped the sun up here," replied Shelly.

"If you must know, they worshipped 'the God of the bogs," said Kit.

Shelly threw him a disgusted look and followed me into the kitchen, "He needs more work," she said, "work keeps him focused."

"There's a letter here for you Norma," she pointed to the table, "with a very neatly typed address." Her voice held a questioning tone. "I don't think it's from Fernando, unless he's paying a flying visit over to England that is."

Warily I opened the letter. For some reason I always felt apprehensive as to the contents of any unknown correspondence.

"Is there a bomb inside?" she teased.

"Of unknown origin," I replied.

After reading the first few lines I felt speechless with surprise, the contents were like a bolt out of the blue...

"Who's suing you Norma?" Shelly thought of everything in a legal structure, her two years work in a solicitor's office made sure of that "According to the rules of law, letters are of two varieties, formal and informal. When formal and served by a solicitor they are most usually after your money, as much as possible."

"I never knew that, but this isn't a threat ..."

"Write back and say you are referring the matter on to your

solicitor, takes months to reply, waiting means time and time equals money," she said returning to her book.

"Nobody wants to sue me," I had to shout; it was difficult to be heard over Shelly when in full flow. "It's an invitation!"

We are holding our two day festival of the horse on the 26th and 27th of August and would be honored to include your beautiful Iberian stallion in our display to music section, with his rider of course! We also extend this invitation to your Irish Draught horse, again in display to music. The following will be included, one bungalow set in the grounds, residence for groom, excellent stabling, dinner and barbecue. Payment is by agreement.

...She raised her eyebrows then smiled, "Just imagine my boy becoming a star! And Donovan too of course, shame about the long drive but everything sounds splendid. The only thing is that I can't go. Kit will have to groom as mum intends driving down to see me, birthday treat I do believe. I love the idea, sounds like the real world to me. None of that damn dressage nonsense. Who wants to see riders entering at A and tracking left at C and then being marked on how neatly they perform the maneuvers? People want entertaining. I'm sure horses find it boring too," she passed the letter on to Kit who beamed with happiness.

"Will you accept the invitation Norma?" he said hopefully "sounds fantastic."

"Of course I accept it. My only worry is Geoff. He doesn't know anything about it … yet." During August Geoff hated travelling anywhere, particularly in the horsebox. August was quite definitely a stay at home month.

"You know what Geoff thinks about going anywhere in August, 'everyone travels in August and I stay at home,' that's what Geoff says."

"Leave everything to me, other than riding and driving of course. I promise you will not have to lift a finger," Kit sounded very definite and was already setting up his persuasion tactics. I could see it in his eyes. "Geoff must be ready for a little holiday. Just leave all the talking to me!" So I did just that and gave Kit the task of pressurizing Geoff into taking his well earned break.

*

Spring slipped into glorious summer … A meltingly hot summer, when our away from it all farm suddenly became the place to visit. From dawn till dusk people from the towns in the valley took this rare opportunity to walk talk or jog over the moor by way of the seldom used footpath which meandered across our land.

Piccadilly Circus had nothing on us, the footpath was free, there were no expensive cafes and the scenery was as good as it gets, breathtakingly so. During the months of July and August our compensations for living far away from civilization became excessive. Geoff said we had earned our just reward for enduring six months of hell.

"Sit back, take it easy and enjoy every minute, winters not far away," he always said. And so I did just that, I settled back to enjoy two months of bliss.

"Why not come out with me?" said Amber. "I think you would love painting and you are on holiday." So I accompanied Amber on painting expeditions and quickly realized why she was passionate about painting the moors. I painted a golden haze scene on a summer evening when the heather cast shadows over the surrounding wilderness. Amber sold five lavender haze paintings in one week on Todmorden market...she sold mine as well, which made me very proud.

The rest of summer was a luxurious long holiday, full of lazy days and incredible sights. I loved the amazing orange scarlet sunsets so vivid and spectacular. We found a nearby waterfall with a crystal clear pool where we swam. All around me there was pure untainted beauty.

When the sun shone brightly there suddenly appeared mammoth sized butterflies that hovered fleetingly over the tiny moorland flowers. Rare moorland butterflies with wings the size of small birds, in colors of the richest hues.

"Moorland butterflies are listed as an endangered species,"

Shelly informed me, "died out years ago in poison spray land."

The total absence of flying insects delighted Shelly, she loathed flies, detested them in fact. In her room was a sonic anti fly device, plus various strips and traps for the one that got away.

"Did you know that flies can't survive long in high treeless areas, where farming, people and sewers have not yet trod? Sue tells me she is being eaten alive by mosquitoes in Seville, sounds appalling. This is the reason why it's so beautifully peaceful up here... except for the footpath."

"Maybe the townies take walks up here to escape the insects down in poison spray land?" I trod carefully taking care not to upset her on the subject of insects. She withdrew from the conversation when anyone became flippant about her terror.

"What sensible people," she agreed.

Unfortunately, it was Ganador who turned the peace into chaos. Regrettably he had retained his old hatred of any hiker carrying a back pack, as well as becoming amazingly skillful in jumping the five barred gate which divided his paddock from the footpath. He would fly through the air deftly landing in any field where any hiker dared to tread. Terrified hikers had no choice but to run for their lives before Ganador evicted them forcibly by throwing them over the handiest dry stone wall and sadly it was only possible to keep him and hikers apart by stabling him during daylight hours together with Fred. So now there were two delinquents in the stable.

As the month of July came to an end with still not a drop of rain, the outlying moor burned for three days like a bonfire. Not surprisingly old overgrown moorland waited for the smallest spark to blaze away. Each time the breeze blew, smoldering reeds sent out sparks that snatched at clumps of heather, spreading the flames outwards towards the farm, searing down into the earth, smoking and cracking along buried peat roots until flames rose up from adjoining fields. On the third day we prepared the horsebox ready to move the horses out. As dense black smoke thickened, the horses coughed and so did we. Just as we were about to load the first horse, a team of fire fighters drove into the stable yard, they dug a moat all the way round the farm and down the boundaries of the fields. They stayed put all night topping up ditches and hosing surrounding moorland.

I will always think of that team of fire fighters as my heroes. Around the farm I heard the agonized cries of moorland birds, the tiny birds which nest on the ground in gorse or bracken simply because there are no trees, their nests destroyed to ashes. The smell of burning peat hung in the air for days and large areas of blackened grass lay scattered over the moors.

After the fires, summer began to draw to a close. I felt the air freshen; the rays of the sun weaken from the very first week in August. High on the moors it was time to enjoy the few remaining weeks of summer before the chill of early morning became a reality. Soon, any warmth from the sun would become merely a memory. Time in summer appeared to pass at a much slower tempo, unhurried and leisurely, not pressing or urgent… it gave me the sort of feeling I wanted to enjoy forever and ever. But I never lost track of number one on the agenda, the date of the display.

Exactly as Fernando had predicted, Ganador's work improved daily and now included oiled transitions between piaffe and passage, lateral movements and canter in place, plus a spectacular Spanish walk. In the exercises of high school Ganador became my teacher. He taught me how the old airs should feel, without any special preparation, the same movements that his ancestors had been bred for.

In the second week of August our displays were done, dusted, passed by Shelly and applauded by Kit. At last the pressure had gone away or so I thought.

"All we need now is the right music, should be a simple matter," said Geoff confidently looking at my varied stack of discs. But a simple matter it definitely was not. After two full days of erroneous musical mix ups Kit came to the rescue with some sound advice from 'Arty,' the circus bandmaster.

"I discussed our little problem with Arty down at circus headquarters. He's given me this advice. You can take it or leave it. 'Forget choreography and rhythm at this late stage. Play Irish music for Irish horses, flamenco for Spanish, Oriental for Arabs. A rule of thumb,' he said. 'Don't ask me why but it always sets the mood.'"

"Arty's correct," I said. "There's only one kind of music for Ganador and that's flamenco, exotic and fiery…"

"Try these cassettes then…" And Kit handed over the circus cassettes, and we followed the bandmaster's rule of thumb creating an arrangement of Irish pipe music for Donovan. I never told Kit that Ganador's flamenco had been chosen by me… not Arty.

"Don't worry about offending Kit," said Geoff. "He doesn't know one note of flamenco from another, plus he's tone deaf."

August the twenty fifth was to prove the longest night of my life; it was also the night prior to our marathon drive down to the display. Throughout the day we packed and labeled boxes which housed all the items deemed necessary for any respectable display horse. After loading my last box Shelly handed me an aerosol spray, name of 'One Puff.'

"You never know what there may be down there," she said very seriously. "Just remember to use it," she cautioned. "Donovan and Ganador are not familiar with insects, could send them crazy."

"Perhaps you have a point," I replied. "The moors have nothing in common with where we are going." I tried to hide any hint of sarcasm.

"What time are you loading?" she asked, already planning her morning routine.

"Geoff needs to be away before eight … cool and unhurried."

"Be difficult to be cool and unhurried when Kit's around."

"Kits sleeping over tonight," I warned her. "Then I can be sure he arrives on time in the morning. Everything has to go perfectly tomorrow morning…"

*

"I snore, or so Mum tells me," Kit informed me that evening. "Let me sleep downstairs." Like a fool I insisted he slept upstairs in the tiny bedroom which directly adjoined ours.

"Mum tells me I have a sleep problem," he said with a smile. I failed to see the warning lights flashing, became deaf to the sound of bells ringing.

"I don't know what it is though because I'm asleep," he said with not a care in the world. "Goodnight everyone," and he was gone.

"You look tired, why not have an early night?" said Shelly. I think she must have spotted my half closed baggy eyes. "You worry for the world Norma."

"I worry for the universe never mind the world"

"Try counting sheep," she advised. "I count crashing waves accompanying the song of dolphins…"

Tranquil and silent described the first hour of slumber. How could it be otherwise? High on the moors noise had no place, especially in summer when the wind could not raise a sigh.

The silence felt rather like floating in the middle of a calm ocean, until my doubts and fears reared their heads. So I counted sheep, hundreds of perfectly behaved, whiter than white sheep, all waiting in line to jump over a wooden stile. Geoff went through his nightly routine of being a dead body "If I stretch out and refuse to move, sleep may possibly come along," he muttered. "Do you think I'm an insomniac?" he asked knowing full well he was upsetting my sheep counting.

And then I heard Kit's sleeping problem, the one he found too difficult to explain. A stream of inarticulate chatter came floating on the air waves out of the confines of the tiny room. Loud, unintelligible chatter we must listen to for the entire night.

This was serious torture- irritating, nerve shattering torture.

"Should I tell him to sleep downstairs with the dogs?" I whispered to Geoff, worrying about his ability to drive over three hundred miles in the morning.

"The dogs would probably kill him," he said furiously. "And I can't say I'd blame them," he added.

I tried to keep calm by focusing on my sheep but counting more than ten proved impossible, just waiting for his next frenzied babble set my nerves on a knife edge.

At exactly three thirty a.m. Kit's alarm bell rang violently; Geoff dealt with this intrusion by arising out of his dead body state to bellow nasty words through the door of the tiny room.

"Sorry Geoff," Kit replied sleepily. "I must have mixed the fingers up," and he immediately began to snore like a train.

This catalogue of disasters finished at six fifteen when Kit tramped through our bedroom pulling his weekend case.

"Slept like a top," he said walking past the bed "must be the quiet." Geoff whose head was under the sheets had yet another little outburst. "If Sue had been here, she would have put your bed in the barn," he shouted to the departing figure of Kit.

It was then I heard Shelly; "Good morning camper," she said in her frosty early morning voice. "I heard some drunken hikers on the footpath last night. Did you hear them?" she asked Kit in a testing manner.

"I went out like a light," he said truthfully. "But I've never heard of drunken hikers before." Kit laughed at the idea of drunken hikers on the footpath.

"Well you have now" she said briskly before descending the stairs.

Shelly always slept peacefully. She drifted away to the rhythm of the sea as she listened to her free cassette with its 'sounds of the ocean,' the one that came taped to her de-tox diet plan. Everything seemed so structured and planned in Shelly's world, nothing unforeseen ever happened, not when she was about.

But she wouldn't be about at the display...

16 The Finest Creature To Ever Walk God's Earth

August 26

By nine a.m. the horses were loaded and the ramp clanged shut. Shelly placed the picnic hamper in the cab, gave Kit a final lecture on preparing feeds and the horsebox pulled slowly up the drive. At last we were off! As we drove along the moorland road I began to have serious doubts about bringing Kit along. Even though I knew his weaknesses, he could constantly shock me by 'forgetting to think'…as he called his not with it moments.

Never did it cross my mind that I would say 'thank the Lord for Kit,' three times in one day… but I did.

Geoff was in a terrible mood, but who wouldn't be after our night of hell and with over three hundred miles to go?

Kits chatter kept Geoff awake, directed him onto our pre arranged route and amused me. If I closed my eyes his voice droned on in the background like the comforting hum of radio four. His flow of chatter never stopped until we arrived at our destination just before 8 p.m.

Geoff and I were shown to our bungalow, Kit to his residence and the horses to the stables. We were exhausted with heads still throbbing in rhythm with the horsebox. Kit however was just coming alive.

"Leave everything to me," said Kit. "You both look as though sleeps calling." And sleep was calling, for we slept for a full ten hours.

The morning of the display was bright and sunny with not a whisper of a breeze. One of those perfect last days of summer when all around is peaceful and still, a wonderful under an English heaven day. And then Kit's cheerful voice broke the calm as it boomed from the bungalows kitchen.

"Morning folks, did you sleep well? I partied until the early hours, it was brilliant! And I met a French circus proprietor who may need a groom, subject to a good reference from you of course," he said hopefully.

This could be a tricky situation. I hated writing references if I wasn't completely sure. The choice was too limited. Did I lie, state the truth or invent something that lay between both?

"I'm doing bacon and eggs for breakfast, horses already seen to, so relax," Kit was always happy he never worried about life. Shelly believed this pseudo happiness was his weakness "Life needs planning and organizing," she always said, "or we put everything around us on standby. One can either act responsibly or be prepared to join the sheep," said Shelly adamantly. "My last boss never tired of this proverb:

'There are those born to lead and then there are the sheep,

But always remember the sheep only listen to the whisperers.'

"Takes a little thinking about Michelle my girl, he would say. Trouble is, I still don't get the message after thinking about it for three long years."

After breakfast we walked down to the stables for yet another surprise. Kit had been hard at work, most probably from the early hours. The horses were magnificently turned out, Donovan's rich bay coat gleamed as never before, his mane skillfully braided into one single plait.

Dazzling was the only word to describe Ganador, red roses accentuated his silver mane. His floor length silken tail shimmered in a spiral of tiny waves with the help of a golden crupper...

"Discreetly borrowed from circus headquarters," said Kit.

"And this is meant for Donovan!" He said proudly. Kit held up a beautiful ostrich feather plume right in front of Geoff's face. "Charlie the high school horse wears it!"

"NO WAY…" Geoff looked shocked to the core at the merest thought of Donovan wearing any ostrich feathers. "He looks eye catching as he is. I draw the line with plaits. This isn't the circus."

"But it's very near to cabaret!" I'm feeling sorry for Kit.

"I categorically refuse," Geoff said flatly. When Geoff uttered these three words, it was the end of the matter. Kit gave a long sigh before turning his attention to me. The ostrich feather plume he put back in a velvet box, labeled 'Charlie.'

"Ganador looks beautiful Kit. Why not put the ostrich plume on him … I give you my permission." He smiled wryly, "Ganador doesn't need any decoration he's beautiful as he is."

Whether Ganador knew he looked splendid I can't be sure, but he seemed to know this day was special. His black eyes sparkled with excitement as he listened carefully to the hum of voices. Perhaps he was reliving the past, the era of his ancestors, those fighting horses of centuries before whose wish was only to serve their master. The mirrored walls in the riding hall simply upheld his conviction. He darted swift stares into each and every mirror whenever he glimpsed his beauty. To Ganador the mirrors held a special fascination allowing him to examine his splendor again and again

"Norma!" Kit's voice disturbed my thoughts, "Your display is on at one or thereabouts. So you've just time to change." His voice reminded me of a highly organized trainer. "And Geoff's on at two," he added, "without plume."

"I thought the plume was gorgeous Kit, but Geoff hates anything over the top."

Kit laughed, "Geoff likes what Geoff likes!" he said tellingly.

On my way back to the bungalow I peeped into the display hall. It's packed to capacity with a lively crowd of all ages. I can feel ripples of excitement in the air and at that moment my stomach jumps, and a surge of fear suddenly swallows me up. I feel scared stiff. The spectators look on with the critical scrutiny of any horsey crowd. Probably they are people who have come along to compare or criticize, maybe to admire. Horsey crowds are never easily won over. Silly thoughts keep racing through my head, I can't stop them.

'What if Ganador starts to do his own thing? What if he puts in some airs above the ground and I fall off?'

As if in a dream I hear Kit's voice, "Almost twelve o'clock and time to get changed. In fifty minutes we wait outside the entry."

At twelve fifty, I'm killing time under the way in sign. I hope Kit comes down, he's got my program. After a few anxious minutes he appears clutching the grooming bag, I feel so relieved.

"Ganador's display music starts following the commentator's intro. You know the rest. Enter - halt at X, and then wait until he stops talking!" Kit tightens Ganador's girth, he places one last red rose in his forelock. "You look lovely," he smiles and squeezes my hand. I feel like hugging him. "Go with the flow!"

The tension is unbearable, but at last the flap is held back ... This is it, there's no going back now.

'I remember entering, and riding straight down the center line the pace is passage, slow and hovering. After halting the lights suddenly dim ... we are surrounded by a circle of sparkling silver. I think its strobe lighting. Ganador's reaction to this surprise is to launch into piaffe. He can't understand the sudden darkness or the lights, so he does what he knows best. He probably feels mixed up, just like I do. My heart starts thudding. It's banging in my ears. Surprisingly it thuds in time with the tempo of my music, and that must be at least one hundred and twenty beats a minute. Damn! Kit told me the music follows the commentator ... Where's he? So I use the darkness to fix a smile. I don't feel like smiling, I'm so nervous. Unexpectedly Ganador rears; I hear voices saying "Oh!" ... They must think the rear is part of the act. He's fed up; he wants to get on with his job.

The music stops ... Right at that moment I hear the voice of the commentator. He's standing next to me, in my circle of lights with his hand on Ganador's neck.

"Ladies and Gentlemen, the most important breed in the history of mankind, the Iberian Horse. He fought our battles, never fleeing from danger. The breed worshipped by Kings and Emperors because of his outstanding beauty and incredible bravery. We bring to you - Ganador V!"

He turns the microphone off ... he whispers, "If you need me I'm behind letter C dear..."

Suddenly the lights come on, and Ganador's impromptu piaffe stops dead. He stands so very still ... Just like a statue. All around me are flashes from cameras. For a split second there's a blinding flash. Dazzling light reflects off a chrome prop. The flash upsets my poise, but Ganador isn't spooked. When the camera people walk away, the lights are dimmed. Now there's total silence, I can hear myself breathing. Any chatter or movement just dies away with the lights.

At that moment I hear the opening bars of our music, a malaguena. It's my favorite. At long last we begin our display.

For the first few minutes we describe shapes, in walk, trot and canter, circles, figure of eights, loop's and serpentines. It's called 'working in.' I double check he's moving forwards in a round shape on both left and right reins. I pray there are no tigers in corners, loose dogs, or sudden movements. Display riding is called 'working an act,' an act that can never be pre-determined. How can it be?

I've a feeling Ganador's enjoying himself by the brilliance of his stride. Each movement is perfectly made, and executed. I wonder if the spectators comprehend how much work we've done to reach this standard. Already he's waved his wand on the audience ... He fascinates people. Maybe they realize he's a King ... A King from a bygone age.

I'm halfway through the routine now. The energy I felt through the morning has just drained away. At this moment I feel fragile, maybe even dizzy. The twirling motion in the pirouettes always has this effect. Now Ganador's gone into his canter changes early ... He's doing three time changes down the long side. I'll just have to go with him. I must dictate the pace! Concentrate, establish the rhythm, and count the strides ... Two, two three - Three, two three. At letter A, transition down to walk, it's a good transition, well balanced, forward going. Neatly through the corner, straighten up, prepare six steps piaffe, one, two and three... He's done it again! He's performing Spanish walk. Maybe his strides are gracious and measured, but I did not give the signal. Ganador is doing his own thing.

So I stop dictating; I sit lightly in the saddle follow his movements and try to smile. I become conscious that the display is no longer in my hands. It's no longer mine to give, Ganador has taken over. Everyone is looking at a first class showman, putting on the display of his life just for them.

So I relax … I feel his taught muscles where once there were none. His back is soft and swings from side to side. How I love this horse. In piaffe, his rhythmic spring feels incredible. He moves forward into passage, his suspension hovers; I could be sitting on a cloud. Once again he's dancing in piaffe. He's about to rear; I sense his weight transfer to his hind legs … panic grips me. Carefully I lighten the rein contact, I must not overbalance him. Slowly he raises his forehand taking his weight on well bent haunches. His classical Levade suddenly changes to a high Gineta rear. A showman to the last!

As the last note of the music dies away, he stands motionless, his silken mane tangled with sweat and red roses. The spectators go wild. I breathe easier…'

Just as we leave the display hall a man of distinguished appearance, in his middle years approaches me. He smiles as he rubs Ganador's nose.

"Well this is a treat Ganador boy! You do look well," the strange man speaks to Ganador. Only as an afterthought does the man turn to me.

"Allow me to introduce myself … Roland, Ganador's first English owner!" So I have finally met Sir Roland. "And you must be Norma?" he asks, still stroking Ganador's nose.

I've a feeling Sir Roland is finding his next words difficult, but I know he wants to say something of importance, something he intends me to hear.

"I want you to know that I never intended Ganador to stay with Adams. I thought the world of Ganador." He sounds surprisingly emotional about Ganador. You'd think he wanted him back. For the very first time he looks me straight in the eyes, the windows of his soul make steady contact with mine, somehow he's making me half believe his last words. "But there were other people to consider." So I let Roland say his piece. He must be feeling guilty; I can hear it in his voice. One moment it's hard, the next sheepish.

"What a relief knowing he's with you, someone who understands the breed and respects him, if you understand me.

When my wife broke her back I sadly let that rascal Adams have him because of his wild temperament," he could not stop talking now. "His full brother Papillon is in my yard, the exact opposite of Ganador. Gentle he is; has a temperament like a lamb. Ganador had a temperament of fire! Always in trouble he was…"

"He's exactly the same now," I said very quickly before the solitary conversation carried on.

"I once found four dead mice lined up in his loosebox. No vermin entered Ganador's box, not if they wanted to live! Struck them dead instantly, he feared nothing." Sir Roland laughed as he relived Ganador's way of dealing with problems. "Only my head groom was capable of handling him, much too clever for the others. Had a nasty habit of striking out with his right fore, frightening he was. Does he still possess this trait?"

"Ganador does not suffer fools lightly and can behave in a territorial manner, if threatened. As to his dealings with mice, he's struck two dead that we know of. Unfortunately they were field mice, a protected species." The moors were not the favored habitat of mice or rats, creatures that much prefer a closer proximity with humans and sewers.

"Anything new or strange angered him," he went on, "I remember erecting a stallion paddock using the strongest timber I could buy. Ganador took one look and began to tear it down as if it were matchwood. Used his teeth he did, before smashing the wood into a pulp by means of striking! I will never forget that day. He was always doing battle… if you know what I mean. I think Ganador was born in the wrong century," Roland said thoughtfully. "If you know what I mean?"

"I know exactly what you mean," I said watching a fragile looking woman wave from the crowd. The one thing he'd not said was how strong Ganador looked. Neither had he mentioned his display, which must have surprised him. After all Ganador had been wild and dangerous.

"Today has been such a relief just to see him again. I never wanted him to go with Adams" He'd said it again, so he must feel guilty. "The man drove me mad he did, calling at the house with his gypsy talk and bidding. But Adams got what he wanted in the end."

Sir Roland patted Ganador one last time. "Look after the boy," he said. "Have to go." I wanted to kick him but that was impossible, so I shouted: 'I read your letter. You wanted rid of Ganador and you gave him to Gypsies to be sold at Appleby fair. To be sold at any cost… all because of your stupid pride." I don't think he heard me because he waved as they disappeared into the crowd, gone forever from my world.

"I heard some of that," said Kit as he wiped Ganador down. "He's not good enough for Ganador."

At that moment I heard a voice behind me, a voice I recognized.

"Tis Ganador; but it cannot be him? The oss you ride reminds me of King Ganador, so he does" the voice said. A man of shabby appearance in the winter of his years staggered towards us. The man continued to stare at the stallion, idly drinking from a can of beer.

His voice rattled ominously. Then he laughed; a frightening hysterical noise before losing his balance and slouching backwards fortunately onto a bale of straw.

The voice was definitely the same as Adams. A drunk and shabby Adams, not the proud dapper man I remembered, but a man on the edge of giving up any pretence of humanity, a tired ill man whose struggles with life were almost over. A putrid odor filled the air round him from the many layers of food that stuck immovably to his clothing. There was no Mother Adams about, I felt sure about that.

I glanced down to his shoes half expecting to see the highly shone impeccable dealer boots the shine of which I could still visualize. I don't know why it is but footwear has a reasonable diagnosis in telling the mental and monetary health of any individual and Adams wore a pair of filthy linen pumps, the soles split apart from the uppers.

This was a man past caring. His hair was not the black immaculately combed hair I remembered, but matted and uncombed under many layers of grease. The smart tweed hacking jacket I remembered so well now appeared no better than a rag, threadbare patches looked one and the same as its material. I asked him how Mother and Mark were faring, but perhaps meaningfully he only heard the name Mark.

"Please tell Mother that Ganador still enjoys his cup of tea" I said thinking that just maybe I could draw him into conversation regarding the whereabouts of Mother, but Adams ignored my words.

"Mark and Evita live in Seville, they do, live in Seville." He said in his rhyming drawl. "Mark has an orange plantation and the finest stables you ever did see. Tis a fact, I tell no lie."

"Mark breeds real classy Spanish horses, beauties they are, fit for a King," he began to laugh, but laughing caused him to cough.

"Wants his Dad to go over he does, but everything seems a struggle, so it does, a real struggle." He stood silently for a few moments as though examining Ganador once more. Ganador's ears flattened back menacingly.

"This oss is not my Ganador," he spluttered, the rattling noises were definitely coming from deep inside his lungs.

"He's a mighty fine creature, but tis not my Ganador, not my lad. My Ganador was a King." It became obvious that he would not be swayed, so I remained silent.

Slowly but deliberately his thoughts returned to the beer tent.

He stood up and swayed drunkenly; holding on to his empty can of beer.

"May luck go with thee lass" said Adams, adding as an afterthought, "When you pass by my palace I'll show you pictures of 'my' King Ganador." Slapping Ganador's neck he made ready to depart. "Finest creature to ever walk the earth," he said turning towards the path that led to the bottom of the field where the 'refreshment' tent was located.

"I'd better be away lass, time to move on," he said staggering down the field.

I led Ganador towards the stables without answering Adams. I was unable to answer, my voice was choked up, eyes blinded with tears. The meeting had begun and ended within fifteen minutes, a tragic meeting with many things left unsaid. His failing voice invaded my thoughts throughout the rest of that day, and even now I sometimes imagine I hear him.

Thankfully Kit's voice broke the silent barrier linking past and present. "Norma, where have you been?" he asked. "It's the parade in fifteen minutes, just time to tidy him up." Kit stared at my disheveled appearance, "Time to comb your hair and do your make up. If you do it quickly," he said as he took Ganador from me. He began work on brushing out his tail and wiping him over.

"Geoff's already in the riding hall, can you hear the Irish music? The spectators' love Donovan… they think he's Spanish!" I quickly carried out his order to tidy myself up allowing Kit to 'do the paint job,' as the circus so aptly calls applying makeup.

"There!" he said proudly, "Magnificent!"

And I rode the finest creature to ever walk the earth into the riding hall…

TEN YEARS LATER.

After ten years had passed we finally made the decision to move away from the high moors. Many tears were shed but there was no alternative for we now had a lovely daughter and no longer could we live on top of the moors where the weather controlled our lives with its blizzards, storms and drifting snow. Driving to school, healthcare and visits to friends were now important daily activities.

Of course, the horses were still our passion. How could they not be? It was heart breaking moving away from the moors, moving away from my enchanted world.

Maybe the feeling was grief, at having lost the home I loved. My heart would always be with the high places, with the hills … With a world that dreams are made of.

When Ganador was almost twenty years of age we returned to the town from whence we came, it was a small town set in a valley where the winter winds blew less fiercely, and where we purchased a pretty small farm standing in one of the last remaining hamlets within the Pennine valley … A place where proper people lived.

It was here that Ganador spent his remaining years together with Fred now aged twenty two and Donovan, twenty five. Although the horses seemed to enjoy the harmony of the lowlands, I never accepted the reality of living away from the moors, feeling inexplicably disconnected from my new life amongst people and society. During the years that followed I missed the magic of the moors and the people who chose to live there with an aching sadness, turning more and more to the teaching of music…my first love.

Often, I thought of Fernando's words: 'I give to you all that I know,' and Manuel's: 'What I give to you is from my heart.' Maybe the time had come to pass on my knowledge … And to remember what mum said about life:

'Life is an adventure that sooner or later comes to an end,
Time is unstoppable…'

17 A Sad Time...

Diary Pendle Valley June 7 1992

'Mum was so right, nothing lasts forever. Sooner or later it comes to an end.

Nuno Oliveira died 1989.

Fernando Sommer d'Andrade died 1991.

The world has lost two of its greatest classical trainers.

How I miss Fernando's letters ... last week I took some of his letters into the music room, I stayed there all day reading them over and over again. Mum tells me I must consider myself fortunate to have known such great men.

'You will never forget them' she said.

'How is it possible to forget them?' I replied...

'It's easy' Mum replied 'When people are not around anymore it's simple to put them out of your mind. Keep their books on your bedside table and read a little every night. Let them speak to you through their words.'

Today is June the seventh, nineteen ninety two and Nunos 'Reflections on equestrian art,' and Fernando's 'The Spanish Horse,' will always have a special place next to my alarm clock.'

Following writing my diary I went downstairs. The first thing I did was throw open the windows. This was the first thing I did every morning, gaze in wonder at the orchard. After my life on the moors the abundance of trees and flowers always took me by surprise. As I looked out, nothing warned me that today was to be the day when my world would begin to fall apart. It was a lovely sunny morning with a feeling of the warmth still to come, a relaxing day.

"Must be the first day of summer," I heard Geoff mutter as he read the morning paper...

"I wonder what the weathers doing up on the moors?"I often pondered on this fact "will it be the same?" I missed the mountain top splendor and the dramatic cloud formations. I missed everything about the moors.

"Definitely not," he said with a trace of sarcasm. "The weather on the moors is most probably chilly and damp, with a topping of thick mist."

If time could stop, I would have stopped it then, on that morning in June watching rays of golden sunlight dancing on the window panes. I don't know how long I remained at the window studying the miracles of nature, for I found my orchard fascinating after sixteen treeless years. But I remember the arrival of the postman and the resounding thud of post upon the wooden floor. Because it was Geoff's day to open the post I sat back and watched as he slammed the household bills down with contempt. Then he opened letter number five, and suddenly became silent; for a moment he hesitated and looked surprised.

"Can you remember looking round a car show in Manchester and entering the prize draw?" he started to smile, looking immensely pleased about something. "Well guess what? We have won the second prize and it's a holiday... a weekend in Spain in a five star hotel!" Geoff's next words rather shocked me "Should we give the holiday away?"

"NO, definitely not," I replied. "This kind of luck is seldom found in the morning post, is it?" The winning of anything like a holiday came as a bombshell. I'd never won as much as a hanky before.

"But who would look after Ganador?" Geoff's sensible voice contained a worried tone. "Let's give it away," he said once more before he handed me the tickets. "Ganador may be long in the tooth but I'd wager he would still win a battle." said Geoff and he was so right.

Ganador was no normal horse, never had been, and never would be. He was a noble battle horse, undeniably born in the wrong century and unquestionably carrying his ancestors spirit of fire. To be honest, he put the fear of God into people. Whenever I rode Ganador out the amazed expressions on faces said it all. People stood outside their houses to watch him pass by, tears rolled down cheeks, children hid behind parents... but no one dared approach him. Everyone marveled at his beauty as he trotted the air... just for them.

By now we had accepted our roles as full time grooms completely, and ever since Shelly departed we avoided holidays like the plague.

"Day trips are much more enjoyable," Geoff would say in the midst of a three hour traffic jam. "Holidays are over rated."

Should there be no alternative but to travel, I went alone. The words: "Is 'he' alright Geoff?" never far from my thoughts, and always the first words uttered. I would sigh with relief on hearing Geoff's reply, "Of course he is." He- denoting Ganador, that miracle of equine creation whose only want was to serve the brave spirit in man, a horse from another age...the age of chivalry and bravery.

But all these thoughts flew out of the window on the morning I chose to follow the route down 'pleasure alley' and to ignore the warning lights flashing 'consequences.'

"The outgoing flight departs at six a.m. Friday, arrival time back in Manchester one a.m. Monday. Ganador will hardly miss us," and I rang Lucy, my part time groom. Lucy knew Ganador well by now and always appeared confident when around him.

"I can," she said, "but only in the afternoons." I had forgotten she had exams. "I finish at one though," she went on, "which gives me time for a sandwich before following on with Ganador."

I remember writing 'afternoons sorted,' and then replacing the receiver. Just as I put down my pen, David the gardener popped his head round the kitchen door.

"Just checking up on coffee time Norma" David always smiled; I could never remember seeing him without a smile.

"Don't you dare move," I said, "because I'm making coffee this very minute" As David sipped his coffee I told him the story of our prize weekend in Spain, I also told him Lucy could only do the afternoon feeds.

"Then I'll see to the lad mornings and lunch. Nothing to it, just leave hay and carrots outside his door, I'll open the door to his yard, fill up his water and feed the dogs at the same time... just leave their food out on the kitchen top." David had a heart of pure twenty two carat gold.

"You are a marvel David," and I hugged him.

"I'll take a look at the other two horses on the field when I feed the dogs. The walk will give the dogs some exercise. You just think about enjoying the weekend!"

By this time I was already on the edge of a nightmare situation, slowly but surely a series of unplanned events had started to happen, pulling me in like a magnet, carrying me along. On that morning I still believed I was making the decisions and doing the steering. Planning was my way of coping with problems; I enjoyed making plans right down to the finest details. I could have said 'Let's give the tickets away. I'm not going on some crazy unplanned holiday. Neither am I leaving Ganador without a friend who understands him. Better wait until Shelly or Kit take some leave.' But I didn't say any of these things. Instead I fell straight into the trap... a trap that was set on the morning of June the seventh.

The luxury weekend set off to a weary start, it was delayed for three long boring hours. But we were enjoying ourselves, or at least I was. Geoff permanently moaned, as the word 'late' was reminiscent of a red rag to a bull in his dictionary.

And so the lazy, fought for, free weekend dissolved away into the chaos of travel. Getting there, finding last year's bikini had shrunk, or I had grown, coping with headaches or tummy upsets, and then repeating the whole ghastly process on the return journey.

"Never again," moaned Geoff as we landed. "Complete waste of time all this day dreaming nonsense. Let's get back to real life." The time was shortly before six p.m. when we got back to real life and walked through our very own front door to a chorus of barking crazy dogs, who no doubt agreed with Geoff.

"David's left a note by the phone" Geoff muttered "he's even taped it to the table" Geoff was already changing into jeans and boots getting ready to see Ganador and walk the dogs down the field. As I looked down the hallway to the large sheet of paper, I think I already knew that something terrible had happened, for I began to tremble with foreboding. On the paper David had listed the numbers of incoming calls followed by three printed words: 'GANADOR NOT WELL coming up tonight. David.'

In what seemed to take minutes but was only seconds I ran from the house following the path that wound through the orchard then into the stables. And there I found him...

Ganador swayed from side to side, his eyes almost closed, his coat steaming with sweat, his body trembling from the effort of standing. His right front leg was stretched far out in front of his body, as he tried desperately to keep his weight off the leg.

I spoke his name and will always hear his soft whicker and see his pain filled eyes. It was as if the heart had gone out of him. At that moment Geoff appeared and took the whole awful scene in. With his usual calm approach Geoff decided on how to help, he never seemed to panic.

"Pointless ringing the vet at this hour" Geoff said softly. "The first thing to do is get him out of this pain."

So I went back to the house and carried up his emergency first aid box. You see Geoff had trained as a blacksmith which authorized him to use pain killing or tranquilizing injections. Injecting straight into the jugular vein he waited three minutes for the sweating to ease.

I began sponging sweat from Ganador's coat but then stood helplessly as I watched the ease in which he applied hot and cold treatment to the stallion's leg.

"He needs two bales of straw," he pointed to the feed room, "Quickly." The sharpness of his voice surprised me. "Two bales," he shouted. In a dream I load the bales onto a wheelbarrow. Surely this must be a terrible nightmare from which I will awaken at any moment? I remember shaking out straw to the height of Ganador's belly, and I can still see him sinking into the deep soft bed his pain relieved.

On returning to the house I rang Ron, only to find the words I wanted to say refusing to be said. My mouth was dry. All my energy gone, just drained away.

"Drink this tea" Geoff ordered as he took the receiver from me.

"Ron's coming before nine a.m. I'm going back to the stables with this anti-inflammatory shot, making sure he spends a peaceful night"

David the gardener arrived a little after ten p.m. just in time for Geoff's third offering of sweet tea and biscuits.

"The Lad looked poorly when I opened the door into his yard this morning," was David's first unqualified statement. "He refused to move, eat or drink, but not knowing the ways of horses and knowing you arrived back today I left a message." I knew David must have worried about Ganador. Concern was stamped all over his face.

"The girl never showed up today so I stayed all day with him. I rang her too, and she said she had other things to do," he paused a moment before going on. "So I waited, but she never appeared." Before he left, David placed a bag of apples on the kitchen table. "Cox's Pippins," he said sadly. "Perhaps he won't say no to one tomorrow…"

18 'Ganador's Last Battle'

June 8 to November 2 1992

It was nine a.m. precisely when Ron arrived at the stables. He quickly assessed Ganador's condition and returned to his car, bringing the cardiac testing equipment into the stables, which surprised me as I expected him to bring his portable x ray.

"Morning Geoff, Norma," he said, quickly followed by a "Good Morning Lads" to the horses in the stables. Ganador replied with a soft whinny. After thoroughly examining the stallion Ron paused and looked at me...

"Norma," he said. "Listen to the stethoscope and tell me what sounds you can hear." And then he asked, "What does the sound remind you of?" This was the first time I had used a stethoscope and I was surprised at the concentration required in order to hear anything at all.

"The sound is of fluid," I replied, "It's similar to an underwater sound, a gurgling noise followed by two softer beats." The tension was unbearable as Ron listened carefully once more. At last he stopped and turned to speak;

"Ganador has suffered a few heart attacks. The result is that the heart is missing beats and his lungs are flooding."

"What can we do?" Geoff sounded stunned.

"Right now I'll give him some drugs which should make him feel much better. The ruptured tendon can be helped immediately though," and Ron began work on the tendon.

"The tendon injury needs six weeks of complete box rest. The heart condition is more serious," Ron looked towards Geoff. "I'm

135

afraid it's something he can't recover from, too much damage has been done."

Ron looked to me now, I could tell by his unusual hesitancy that there was something he did not understand, or found difficult to say. Then at last he spoke.

"Has he been galloped hard or used for anything very strenuous?" I stared at him incredulously, but could see he already knew the answer. I told him the story of our weekend away and the quiet three days Ganador had spent with David and Lucy. From the corner of my eye I saw him grimace when I mentioned the girl's name.

"I know you treat your horses with exceptional care Norma, especially this Lad," Ron's voice sounded restrained.

I think Geoff broke the tension in his usual levelheaded manner "What are his chances Ron, I mean, how long has he got, and is he in much pain?" Ron's expression said it all.

"He's on borrowed time Geoff, a few months maybe, but, he is not in any pain. However, he can never be ridden again; even trotting is too great a strain on him, his circulation is impaired." I remember closing my eyes then feeling Ron put his hand over mine.

"If he attempts to trot he will fall, collapse, call it what you will." Ron adored Ganador, called him his King. Ever since our move to the lowland Ron had been our vet, he was trusted implicitly by all the animals and ourselves.

I remember listening to his soft welsh voice arranging Ganador's medication with Geoff. Before Ron left, he hesitated for a moment and then turned towards me…

"Would you mind if I called in to see the Lad Norma, whenever I'm in this area that is? I have two students who would love to meet him." Then almost in a whisper he said, "And when you feel he's stopped enjoying life, ring me." Ron squeezed my hand and I felt numb with shock.

I wanted to speak but my words refused to be spoken. I wanted to run but could not move. Geoff guided me to the house, pulled out a chair and said quietly, "He's had a good life Norma."

That night sleep bypassed me, as it did for many weeks, as it still does.

Lucy's words kept ringing in my head.

"Can I look at Ganador's Pedigree Norma?"

"Why? It's written in Spanish, and so are the names"

"If ever I buy a horse I'm giving it a Spanish name." Like a fool I fell into her trap. I opened the desk drawer and handed her the papers "What lovely sounding names."

"I'll write some of them down for you," and I wrote down 'Hosco' - 'Nevada' - 'Primeroso...' I signed his death warrant with my own hand. Gave away all his breeding information, to go and show his incredible lineage to the travelers. But if my guess was correct, they were not content with using him. They borrowed him to pull one of their racing traps, until his tendon ruptured, until his heart could beat no longer. When he was wet with sweat and hardly able to move he was discarded, just like an old rag. They walked away without a care in the world. Now all they wanted were good foals to sell at Appleby fair. Towards dawn I didn't want to live in this sick world anymore ... this place where friends betray you.

*

Ganador was to live for six more months. During the mornings he would graze in the orchard, where I loved to watch him from the kitchen window ... For every day was precious. In the afternoons he returned to his stable where a deep bed of straw awaited him, he slept so very frequently. Not once did Ganador attempt to trot within those final six months. Maybe he knew that his days of 'trotting the air' were no more.

Each morning he would come to the kitchen window calling out in his soft melodious whinny, the music of which never ceased to thrill me. With his nose pressed onto the glass, his breath would form patches of steaming mist as he waited for the highlight of each day, his morning cup of tea. Ganador's tea was served with milk and sugar, and given in a china cup from which he sipped. After his tea he proudly walked into the orchard to graze for a while. When David worked in the garden Ganador followed his every move, he trusted David, adored him in fact. David brought him juicy treats and talked to him, he was a friend.

One morning however, after the passing of six months, Ganador decided it was time to give up. He stood quietly in a corner of his box, his eyes almost closed. Ganador was beaten, his strength and spirit gone. Tired and weary he knew he had reached his end.

How do you ring the vet to say your magnificent stallion is fighting his last battle? But somehow I did. I went to the phone with a sense of unworthiness to him.

"I think Ganador's near the end..." these were my words. There was no need to say any more.

"I'll be with you at nine in the morning," his soft welsh voice replied, and I put down the receiver with a terrible feeling of having betrayed a loyal friend.

At nine a.m. the following morning Ron arrived. After listening to Ganador's heart he told me what he could hear.

"The heart is failing Norma, a few more days, perhaps only hours." And so we returned to the house in order to make a plan, a plan to end Ganador's life without his knowledge and in the kindest possible manner. Ganador had ceased to be, he would have wanted this.

Ganador did not appear to notice as Ron injected the sedative, he was so very tired. We waited a full twenty minutes to be completely sure of maximum results before leading him down the passageway on this his final walk. Geoff led him so very slowly - step by step. Daughter Samantha walked at his right side, I his left. Ron stood waiting outside. In the entryway I touched his silken mane for the last time. Ganador had a look of complete exhaustion, he wanted only to sleep. His wavering figure halted upon the grassed area which lay in front of the stables, and Ron gave the final injection.

Within moments Ganador lay dead at our feet, his long silken mane like a fan across his snow white body. Even in death he appeared beautiful, perhaps more beautiful than in life. It all seemed like a fading dream. Ganador gone... part of my life vanished forever. Everything I knew and loved faded away, into what?

No one moved, we all stared at his splendor. I think we all knew this was our last chance to see a noble battle horse ever again. I turned and walked back to the house, I could not bear to watch his body taken away, let the men do that. I wanted to remember him as he had lived, to hear his melodious stallion calls and see his awesome statuesque figure.

Ganador had portrayed a vanished world. A bygone age of splendor and bravery when horses were noble and men were daring. He had breathed the spirit of that age into the lives of all who saw him. Ganador was born in the wrong century.

'With the same courage and pride with which they carried their master into battle, so they carried him out of the foray and saved his life. Then, they lay down to die since the spark of life had left them sooner than their courage.'

Master of the King's Horse, Jaques de Soleysel 1664

19 Finding Out…

Pendle Valley April 8, 1994

Eighteen months had gone by since Ganador's passing. The date was April the twenty eighth and the hour twelve noon. Both figures are stamped indelibly on my heart as being the moment I lost my trust in humanity.

It was a bright spring morning and life had more or less returned to normal, though the word normal now represented the color of pale grey and not shining silver. Ganador's loose box, cleaned and painted was home to "Primero," our three year old Andalucian stallion. Primero had to some extent taken the place of Ganador and of Fred who died only three months later with a stroke. Geoff was busy exercising our new addition on the arena when I heard the voice of David.

"Time to prune the old holly tree," he said changing the blade in his wood saw.

"Take care, David," I said watching him balance the saw on his shoulders before climbing onto the first step of what looked to be his very oldest rickety ladders.

"Never let me down yet. Shout me when coffee's ready Norma," he started up his saw preparing to remove a lower branch.

With a feeling of getting in the way of work I walked over to the front gateway for the post. As I shut the box I looked down the lane towards the town. It was then I sighted distant figures; two men leading horses. The men turned into the lane from the nearby allotment pathway, a distance of three fields away. I don't know why but I felt compelled to stand and wait for them to pass by. A

140

sense of 'de je vu' held me to the spot, deep inside I knew I had seen the same scene, the same movements before.

As the men drew closer, I saw the horses were but colts at weaning. What surprised me was their beautiful color, for both were of glowing silver with the finest silken manes and a proud way of suddenly turning their heads as if to listen to sounds that were audible to them and not me.

Silently, I stood beneath the sycamore tree, listening to the sounds of their musical whinnies, every note so clear and distinct. A magical sound that had been Ganador's alone, a melody I knew so well. When they came to within a short distance from where I stood I saw the leading colt's eyes, enormous black staring eyes.

At that moment I felt chilled to the very core, for I looked into the eyes of Ganador.

Despite my stillness the younger man seemed aware of my presence and paused by the gate. He had all the appearance of the group of people we call travelers, and was no more than a boy.

"Morning lady," he said touching his cap. "Colts are off to Appleby so as to be ready for the Fair." The boy looked to be no older than his early teens, probably father and son I thought.

"Are the colt's for sale?" I asked. He nodded in a childlike manner. I could see tears in his eyes. "I wonder who will buy them…"

"Only the Romany's buy spirited osses lady."

"Who owns the colts?" My voice trembled.

"We do lady," the older man intervened. "A local girl owned the stallion"

The conversation quickly ended when David's saw blade hummed, followed by a branch crashing to the ground.

The young horses responded to this noise by rearing high above the men. Long elegant legs thrashed the air as if challenging all around them. Both colts seemed entirely undominated by the men, who anxiously stepped to the side, away from any danger.

"Silly brainless oss," shouted the father, jerking angrily on the stallion chain. "I'll sell him to the first decent bidder. Dangerous he is… dangerous."

Wet with sweat the dangerous one slowly descended from his rear. But then he tried another attack on the man's patience and refused to move forwards, all the time he watched the man out of the corner of his eye. The red faced man moved to the front of the colt and still he shouted.

"Bloody sod of an oss," he cried out in what seemed to be despair. The terrified young horse wanted to be away and tried to run backwards, he didn't trust the man. He despised him.

I watched the colt staple back one ear, leaving the other forwards, and remembered how Ganador would bluff Adams before he took a bite. Maybe this colt was only waiting his chance? And then I saw his plan. But the man was totally unaware and lifted his hand in a final endeavor to pull the colt forwards. Quick as a flash the colt lunged towards the hand, bit hard and sprang backwards. Holding his head high the colt trembled, waiting to be whipped. He refused to look at the man's fury, for this he had witnessed many times before. The young stallion would only allow the man to see his great courage, never anything less. His eyes stared high above the man's head, as though looking over the horizon. There was a glazed expression deep in his eyes that told me the youngster had switched off. This was his way of dealing with the man, to mentally remove himself from any pain. Now the man could no longer hurt him.

"Crazy oss has messed me up," screamed the man as he unleashed his cutting whip. I watched blood running from his fingers slowly dripping into puddles of rain water. "I'm teaching the sod a lesson so I am."

The boy hastily attempted to calm his father; he'd seen his father whipping colts before and knew his father could never teach this young horse a lesson.

"Don't beat him dad. Take mine dad. He's a sensible one. Good as gold he is" The boy pleaded with his father holding out the leading rope of the sensible colt towards his left, blood free hand. And the man obeyed his son and handed him the dangerous one.

I felt the kind of anger I'd never felt before, an anything goes type, it seared through my body ... I could have killed the man. But what was the point? Ganador had gone. So I watched the men and colts... the strange mix of beauty and lowliness walk away up the unmade track to the place of their departure. As they passed the gateway I saw the dangerous one come alive, his energy renewed. He had won the battle, and was happy to be rid of his enemy. Proud once more he moved off in a stately passage, his body soaring high into the air. His strides seemed to float then to hover until the earth below him became of lesser importance than the air around him.

He 'trotted the air' in the same Kingly manner of Ganador. The same feather light air born passage I remembered so clearly. I could not bear to watch any longer, I felt broken inside. Memories of Ganador came flooding back, I heard his melodic whinny singing out over the valley and I remembered his awesome charisma.

At that moment everything changed. My only wish was to escape... to get away from that pretty hamlet in the lowlands. I had no idea where I wanted to go, perhaps back to the moors. Joyful memories of life on the moors would never be forgotten, and neither would the honesty and kindness of the moorland community. But here within civilization I had found only unhappiness and greed.

So I went back to the kitchen where I found Geoff sitting at the table. He stared down, fingers drumming on the wood, fists clenched, knuckles white.

"I know, I saw it all" he said slowly, his every word heavy in despair "Pity about the company she kept."

"I trusted her..."

"Can't go through life without trust," Geoff placed a cup of tea on the table, his answer to everything.

After the tea drinking ritual he said, "Why not exercise Primero? He only had ten minutes of freedom before those Gypsies walked past, exploded when he saw the colts."

So I led Primero out onto the arena where I stood very still and let the sun warm my back. The heat felt heavenly across my shoulders, and I began to relax a little... never imagining what was to take place next.

20 Estepona Pueblo

Pendle Valley 1998

From that day, my main fixation in life was to escape, my only difficulty, Geoff's unwillingness to even consider the matter. Geoff believed in trying his hardest to make life work out. 'Better the devil you know,' he would say.

He loved his home and craved to put down roots... 'Of fixed abode,' could have been Geoff's middle name.

I on the other hand felt trapped, I had to get away...without Ganador's magic, life had no purpose and was not working out. Within this lovely hamlet, this place where proper people lived, I'd found only greed. The magic of the high places had gone away, been replaced by disorder, the chaos of the lowlands. Here, I felt no closeness, no real friendship, just self indulgence on a massive scale. And when life was not working out, wanderlust crept in...I wanted to search for a horse like Ganador, for there must be one, in some corner of Europe.

Whenever Geoff said, "the sun always shines on the next valley," he tested my powers of persuasion to their limit.

"Well maybe it does," I'd reply leafing through a heap of property magazines, casually I would throw him pictures of azure seas, or Spanish horses galloping along dazzling white beaches. If that didn't have the desired effect I followed up with castles standing on cliff tops as if by magic, and villages winding down to the ocean.

"The grass is always greener on the other side of the fence," he always said before moving my offerings back from where they

144

came. But then fate took a hand in the persuasion of Geoff, fate in the form of vandalism. It all started when the farm next door applied for rezoning, from green belt to future building land. This brought furious opposition, which in turn created strong public and media interest in our unheard of lane. Angry groups of protestors marched up and down the footpath, only stopping to take photographs of the trees.

"List the trees," they shouted. "Keep the green." I wholeheartedly agreed with them, but in their eyes... we had the label of fellow conspirators.

The first frightening episode was the firing of our hay barn. It took place one bright Saturday morning when I was alone in the stables. Geoff and Sam were out shopping. The last thing I remember is lifting a brush to sweep the long alley way between loose boxes. A job I never carried out, as a deafening explosion ripped the brush out of my hands and threw me to the floor. When I dared look over the stable door, flames blew fiercely across the entry way, I could feel the heat, smell the unmistakable stench of smoke.

'I have to get out-' But the horses?

'I have to reach a phone- and there's only one way... through the fire...'

In those few seconds, the noise suddenly began exploding all around me, not big like the first explosion, but short and sharp like machine gun fire, though strangely only two horses appeared to panic. Wetting a towel, I wrapped it round face, upper body and hands, and ran for my life. Colliding with a fence I turned a somersault, only then did I realize I was out. Running to the house I grabbed the phone and dialed.

'Emergency,' a voice replied.

'Fire,' I screamed.

'Where are you?' the voice asked.

I became silent. My address had gone away.

"I can't think," I whispered into the phone.

'Don't worry,' the voice said. 'We have your address. I'm sending a team out now.'

On running back to the stables I saw the fire had miraculously stayed the same, it was definitely no worse. And then I saw why. A passing hero had seen the flames and climbed onto the stable roof. He stood hosing the stables long wooden side, preventing the flames from spreading further.

Only minutes later a fire engine drove into the yard and put out the fire. The hay barn was there no more, just a smoking bonfire within a war zone, or that's how it looked.

That night, the police visited me with news of their findings. Two neighborhood children had caused the blaze, a five year old and a seven year old. The officers said they had 'spoken to them sternly.'

Other mindless acts of vandalism were to follow the fire. The pretty wooden gateway became the next target for attacks as it stood on the farms footpath. Following attack number three on the gateway, carried out by a man with an iron pole, Geoff spoke the words I longed to hear, "Let's move to Spain," he said in his slow factual voice. "Cuts all the flying out…"

"Are you sure?" I said in a measured way hoping to conceal my delight. "What changed your mind?"

"Because it's warmer," he said adamantly as he buttered his toast. I was ecstatic with joy and lost no time in putting the farm up for sale.

So Geoff chose the country and location, he loved the hills above Estepona Pueblo in the southernmost part of Andalucia. It's a place where time by the clock has no meaning, where sleek caballos abound and bewitching landscapes are waiting to be found around every corner. It's a place where life passes by on a hot bed of sizzling Spanish culture. And in a strange way it reminds me of the Yorkshire moors, an enchanting place within a foreign land, where once more I can experience freedom…

Geoff found a lovely finca, surrounded by pine trees yet with incredible views over the Mediterranean Sea. From my terrace I gaze at the sun rising above the sea, leaving steps of golden light upon its shimmering surface. At night I gaze at mysterious pathways of stars across the heavens, it's a time when the finca glows silver under the light of the moon. Our finca nestles in the foothills of the rugged Sierra Bermeja Mountains. On the coldest days of the year, I see snow sparkling on its summits and on clear days in summer, the coastline of Morocco. In the distance I see Gibraltar, where the story of Ganador's ancestors began, where the last piece of genetic code was brought over by the invading Islamic army of Jebel Tarik. The final bit of DNA which completed the genetic profile of the Battle Horse of King's and created the most supreme combat horse in history.

All around the finca are lemon and orange plantations. The local farmers say the location is a 'miracle of nature' where fruit is harvested not once, not twice, but three times a year. Mother would have loved the finca, but she's not here anymore...

Diary April 2000

Mum died this morning, it wasn't a shock. She had come to the end of life. On her final day, when she saw me walk towards her bed, she smiled, but only in her eyes. After some hours, she fell into a deep sleep. I went for a coffee, when I returned Mum was no more. She always said it was easier to depart this life with no one around. Never will I see her lovely smile again, feel her touch or hear the softness of her voice, never...

21 The Crown of Seville

October 8 Cortijo Reinoso Andalucia 2002

After the first hot summer had passed, I waited until the rain came and the sun scorched Andalucian earth started to show early signs of life. Maybe it was this 'miracle of nature' that caused the inevitable to happen ... I started to crave once again for a horse whose ancestors had carried a King.

I knew I would never find another Ganador but there was no harm in looking around.

In the end I stopped listening to reason, I gave in and listened to my heart. One morning I picked up the phone and rang Pepe. I had to know the truth about Ganador, the crown of Seville and Mark. And Pepe held the key.

"Twelve years too late" Geoff looked at me doubtfully and frowned "Life moves on ... he won't be there now" But he was there, he answered my call ... recognized my voice. So we arranged to meet in Sevilla's old town the following Monday morning at nine thirty prompt. He suggested a café overlooking the river close to the Puerto de Triana.

"Take a taxi" he said "Park at the station"

I arrived at nine ... the taxi found the way. The café was called Pepe's Rendezvous, inside it was cool and dark with a private feel about it. The only seats were sturdy wooden benches, the flooring faded terracotta tiles. In a way the bar reminded me of The Shepherd ...it had no pretence - it didn't need any, already it hummed with life. The walls around the bar were covered with photos of Spanish Horses and flamenco artists. In the corner of each was a name …Nevada … Jubiloso …Glorioso, names I knew by heart. There must have been at least two hundred photos, maybe more; the walls were papered in history. I stood by the wall covered in photos of Spanish Horses, I ordered a coffee. The waiter asked if I wished to sit in the courtyard. He gestured to a high arched doorway it led to a pretty patio. It was Moorish in design with lush plants, orange trees and vines surrounding its high walls. I sat in the shade close to a fountain and listened to a classical guitarist playing the Adelita by Tarrega. The delicate fragrance of orange blossom floated in the air, sweet and lingering …

And then I heard his voice … half sung, half spoken. The melody of the Gitano's of Sevilla.

"Buenos Dias Senora,"

"Bien … Muy bien," I'd forgotten how dramatically handsome he was. He'd dressed in the manner of a rich Romany Gitano. All in black, his hair swept back into a pony tail ... gold crucifix, gold earrings, gold rings. A few strands of grey now showed at his temples, his wrinkles were deeper … but he hadn't changed much.

A waiter fussed around the table in a deferential manner, Pepe lifted his hand, the waiter walked away.

"It's been a long time?" So he still spoke a gentile English, and I wondered where he'd cultured the accent.

"Nineteen years Pepe," he kissed my hand and slid his arm around my shoulders. He gestured to a table at the opposite side of the patio, it was laid for breakfast. There were two chairs, they were soft and quilted nothing like the wooden benches.

We sat under some orange trees - sunlight shimmered on the fountain, its tiles dazzled me with mesmerizing geometric designs rotating in symmetries of space and color. The setting could have been a dream.

After coffee, he sat back in his chair and closed his eyes "Perfecto" he said dreamily. The haunting sounds of guitar music whispered as one with cascading water from the fountain. Perfect was the only word.

"So you are looking for a horse?" he suddenly asked "A horse like Ganador …" Why had his question taken me by surprise? He

149

was only being honest.

"In a way I suppose I am, but I know I'll never find another Ganador…"

"As long as you understand that," he raised his eyebrows and I felt sure he looked sad, as though he didn't want to hurt me, didn't want to spoil my dream.

"I can't stop longing for another horse Pepe; it must be Spanish and possess just a few of Ganador's qualities." He leaned forwards and put his hand over mine.

"The breeding of Ganador was very special. His ancestors once carried Kings. But today's Kings drive in cars. Noble battle horses like Ganador are no longer needed, no longer wanted." He shook his head; he looked more relaxed now he'd told me what he wanted to say.

"But I feel that I have to search," I whispered.

"Searching is good … Seeking out is sometimes impossible."

The haunting sounds of classical guitar abruptly changed to fiery flamenco … Rolling chords moved through recurring changes of tempo, wild, gay and more Gitano than any music I had ever heard before. Complex cascades of notes rose and fell before coming to rest within lingering discords. Pepe listened in rapture to the music. The waiters stood as if hypnotized under the arched entryway, they clapped, but not with regularity, there was a second rhythm a counter rhythm, known only to them … The unmistakable rhythm of a Bulerias … dramatic, inspired and entirely unchoreographed.

"Espiritu!" shouted Pepe. Enthusiastic oles rang out from his audience. The mood felt euphoric, I'd never felt such intensity. But then the magic ended, the waiters returned to their work, the guitar became soft and languorous, as if the flamenco had never happened.

"You like the music?" he asked, the evocative sounds of flamenco caused me to slip into Spanish.

"Me gusta mucho…"

"Student del Colegio de Sevilla…"

Tongue in cheek, I asked if Gypsy flamenco was also a subject in el Colegio… he laughed and said "No!" Shaking his head vigorously he said, "Only flamenco classical."

"Of course," Why hadn't I thought? Flamenco 'puro' would present insurmountable obstacles to any musician, due to one simple fact: To transcribe gypsy flamenco to manuscript would be virtually impossible because of its complex improvisation.

After the applause it was time to go…

"La Yeguada!" He smiled and we walked through the photo lined bar and down towards the river where he'd parked. People were crowding into the area … queuing for riverboats, visiting bars and cafes, others stood talking … some sat on a wall overlooking the river. For a moment I imagined I saw suspicious glances, people staring then moving out of our way. Maybe Gitano's were held in low esteem in Spain, the same as in England, the same as everywhere in the world.

Pepe's car was a top of the range Mustang, its color was black. What color did I expect? The number plate shouted PEPE 101. Thick dark windows gave a clue to the rest … in the bottom corner of each was a tiny makers logo, it said 'Armstrong Glass.' Such an insignificant detail, but I knew its implication.

"The most reliable bullet resistant glass," Billy had once told me. "We call it transparent armor. All M.D. transport comes automatically equipped, as do the ministry offices." And now I was staring at it.

As he opened my door he bowed, exactly like Adams used to bow, right hand across his heart. He took his seat behind the wheel, and pulled into the traffic flow with a screech of engine noise. I felt excited … At last I was about to see the Yeguada where Ganador had been bred. Perhaps today would allow me to put his memory away forever, to close the book labeled Ganador.

First, Pepe crossed over the Puente de Triana, driving along the wide callé by the river, up into the old town, handling the maze of narrow streets as only a local could. Weaving in and out, pointing to famous buildings. Once more he crossed the river. This time over the Puente de San Telmo … suddenly he turned right and stopped the car.

"Look!" He extended his arm towards La Giralda mosque tower.

Now I gazed across the river at the cathedral and La Giralda. The horizon was limitless. Rays of sun cast glinting lights on the water, gleaming lights of many colors.

"The view's beautiful Pepe…"

"The sunlight of the night…"

"Sounds like poetry"

"When the moon fades, hints of daylight glimmer on its rooftop. Then I know it's time to bolt the door and go home. The minaret of the mosque gazes down over all Sevilla…"

For a few minutes the world stood still … I watched riverboats sailing down to El Arenal port, listened to the sounds of their mournful horns, heard the noises of Sevilla coming alive and breathed the heady scent of orange blossom … So delicate, yet so sweet. There was no hurry, this was a special day.

After a few minutes we were on our way once more, back to the wide callé by the river, heading south of the city, past the Palacio de San Telmo - the Universidad - Parque Maria Louisa. Soon we left the vibrancy of the city behind. When we reached the city's outskirts he put his foot down, acceleration pinned me to the back of my seat. The only sound was of the engine whining, buildings became hidden by trees, objects began flitting past, merging one to the other.

When he slowed down, I wondered why…

"Speed cameras," he said as if reading my thoughts.

"Where are we heading?"

"La Campina …" he answered "Where else?"

In the distance I see a village standing on a low hill. It looks ancient, possibly Roman.

We pass a cottage immediately followed by a gatehouse, he lowers gear, the brakes scream. He turns into a driveway. There's a sign, it reads: 'Prohibida la entrada a toda persona'

An electronic barrier clangs open, he drives in. The entryway is lined by high stately palms. At the top and almost hidden from view is a country lane, "La Campina," he said wistfully. "My paradise …" The view is incredible, orange groves and meadows lay to either side, as far as I can see.

"Todos, Mark y Evita!" Proudly he waves his arm from left to right. Now the road has narrowed, he's forced to drive more carefully; thickly planted cacti form a fierce looking hedge at either side. At last something has slowed him down, if only a little.

"La Yeguada, aqui," He stops the car and waits outside the most splendid gates I have ever seen. Here … right before me, is the inscription of the crown of Sevilla. Not once but several times I see the brand that was Ganador's. It forms the centerpiece of each carefully worked scroll. The seven peaked crown over a script written S, enclosed in a heart shaped coat of arms. I swallow hard as memories of Ganador come flooding back.

The gates open, Pepe drives briskly down the driveway through a long avenue of old and very tall eucalyptus trees. At the bottom of the driveway stands a white mansion, an incredibly beautiful Yeguada. This is the Spain I never knew existed, where the wealthy and privileged live, where families own thousands of hectares of land and unimaginable riches.

"Mire…" he said. I gaze out at numerous paddocks where mares and foals graze in the lower meadows. Pepe sweeps up to the mansions entrance … A small child jumps up and down shouting 'Grandpa, Grandpa.' Pepe swings the child round, I hear them laughing. And then I see Mark walking down the steps of the mansion … He looks exactly the same as he had on the last night I'd seen him in Seville. Young and handsome, his eyes twinkle and never appear serious. His blue-black curls are still shoulder length. Only his clothes are different … expensively so, silk suit all in black but undeniably classy. I wonder if he ever wears his Gypsy clothes …

"It's been a long time Norma" Strangely he greets me in the manner of a fellow Gypsy, elbows touching, thumbs on top, and then he bows ever so low. "Where's my old friend Geoff?"

"Looking to the horses…"

"He's a good Lad is Geoff."

"I know"

"I heard about Ganador's tragic end over at Appleby fair, one of the lads told me … there'll never be another Ganador. That stallion should have been kept here, not sold to England." He took my hand and we walked inside, past enormous Romanesque pillars which signified the main entrance. "You'll need a break after Pepe's speeding!" I follow him into the salon.

The room is impressive ... high ornate ceiling, marble pillars, antique olambrilla tiled floor, each star as blue as the sky. Sunlight danced and shimmered on the French windows. There's a breakfast terrace, it must be the same one where Ganador displayed his brilliance, and lost two grooms their jobs. The view lay over meadows where young stock grazed. I look around me, what I see can only be described as eclectically furnished, sparse but pleasing, each piece carefully chosen, or perhaps inherited ... fine antiques mingle with handpicked modern. Over a late breakfast, Mark told me of his parents,

"Mothers back in Ireland so she is, although she spends her winters here."

He took a deep breath, what he was about to say hurt, "Dad died some twelve years back, on the heavy stuff so he was…"

"I saw him; he was at one of Ganador's displays. He asked me to call into his palace to see photos of 'his' Ganador, the genuine Ganador. He refused to believe the horse I rode had once been his. Your Dad looked near his end, a sad sight."

"You know all about it then, but he still sat in his chair under the stars, right up to his last day. Although I have to admit that his home was no palace. But I did what I could. I paid the staff from the big house to care for him, or he'd have gone long before he did."

So I took the bull by the horns and asked the big question.

"How did you come by a place like this Mark? Must be worth millions…" There, I'd said it, for a moment he was silent, and then his eyes twinkled.

"What's money Norma? Can't buy happiness, but to answer your question Antonio left everything to Evita"

"Who's Antonio?"

"He cleared off with Mariapi, but if you really want to know … Antonio is Evita's biological father, an Italian Count no less and one of the wealthiest land owners in or around Sevilla. The pair had no alternative but to leave Sevilla. Romany law is sacrosanct so it is." And I thought of Mothers words on the evening before Mark and Evita's wedding.

'The Romanies and tradition are one, they will never be parted. Outsiders never fit in with travelling life, or its people. When a Romany woman goes off with an outsider she can expect to be cast out of the clan, and so can her family.'

"I still don't understand."

"How can you when you're not Gypsy bred? Every Gypsy woman grows up knowing the rules." Now I understood the unwritten rules only too well.

"But Evita's lost a mother, Pepe a wife," I said to Mark.

"Can't live between two worlds ... Mariapi crossed the red line that separates Gypsy from outsider. As far as the clan was concerned Antonio stole her from Pepe. They were already mocking Pepe, even daubed his carriage with paint so they did." So now I understood why Mariapi had decided to leave and bring an end to all the whispering, all the hating.

"Maybe one day Evita will go and see her mum. She never stops thinking of her, adored her she did"

"Where did Antonio and Mariapi meet?"

"The aristocrats visit the class flamenco bars when they need someone to love. The Peña's give all the cover they need, I suppose the fiery music and beautiful women do the rest."

Why hadn't I seen the link before ... read between the lines? Romany flamenco, interpreted romance and passion more effectively than any other form of music. Primary instincts that present day society controlled so well - blazed forth with primitive savagery, fervor even. The Gypsies had kept alive a style of music, primal and archaic perhaps, but sensually alive which but for them would have disappeared.

"But how can a mother leave her daughter?"

"Best thing she could have done in that situation. Mariapi didn't want ill fortune wished on her family, so she left."

"How about seeing La Cuadra, the stallion yard?"

"I'd love to ..."

"Then follow me," We walked over the terraces at the side of the main entrance, "Jump in Lass." He pointed to a golf buggy. "Easier than walking, so it is. The stallion yard stands higher than the house, cooler for the osses."

I followed him into the stable yard, a groom shouted out orders, when he saw me he bowed then disappeared from sight. In the yard were four high Palm trees, one in each corner. In the center stood a magnificent fountain, it was marble with carved figurines of horse's heads.

"My favorite yard, only the stallion's are housed here … Feels like home it does." He left the door open which led to the stables and the perfume of sweet meadow hay filled the air.

"Have you any stallions similar to Ganador?" He smiled and shook his head.

"You won't find another Ganador Norma… The old Spanish Oss isn't a buyer's choice anymore. No wars to fight today Lass. People want a horse they enjoy riding that has forward going paces and a good temperament. There's still no more natural sight here in Andalucia than a good horse under an expert rider, and that's the type of horse we try to produce, we must make a new start." Maybe he's correct. Why should anyone want a battle horse? What was the point?

"Evita wants to show you the boys… she'll be back any minute …Take your time …If you want me I'll be in the grooms room"

Just inside the entrance to the stables is a small room with a desk. There's no doorway, just an arch. It's walls are lined with photographs and paintings of the stud's most famous stallions, I stared in awe at some of the finest Spanish lines … Nevada, Hosco, Glorioso, Mexicana, Destinado, and to my astonishment there was Ganador with his brother Papillon. In that instant, I remembered the terrible happening at the breakers yard and what had occurred for the pair to be sold as driving horses to England. Mark was correct when he said 'Ganador should never have been sold.' After all, who would dream of selling a direct descendent of Kings?

Back in the yard, the tranquil calm changes to activity, I hear the ringing of iron shoes on stone cobbles, the footsteps of a groom running past the window. He shouts words too quick to understand. I stand in the doorway. My eyes glued to the approaching horse ... My feelings are probably like a fly on a wall, as I await Evita's arrival.

The horse she rides is a magnificent bay stallion; his coat shines a rich mahogany, his mane and tail are like falls of black silk. She halts close to the fountain. A groom stands by the horses head as she dismounts. Evita seems smaller than I remember. When she turns, I see her flashing eyes, her girlish smile, her arrogant way of moving, and then I hear her voice. She speaks in the same rich Andaluz as does Pepe, half sung ... half spoken. I know the sound so well, its pattern and lilt. The haunting sound of the Gitano's of Sevilla, richly melodious and satisfying to the listener, as though it fulfills a basic need. After all, speech has no need to sound flat, as if a monotone? Why could it not be musical? The groom asked if she wished the stallion to be bedded on veruta or paca.

"Paca," she replied, and then out of politeness asked him if straw was the better choice.

"La paca muy bien señora, mucha mejor."

I tried to calculate her age. She must still be in her twenties, one of the advantages of an early wedding, although she could have passed as a teenager. Her riding clothes are meant to be admired; from her stylish white shirt to the shining brown leather riding boots with the mark of the crown of Sevilla stamped exactly at the knee, the place where the maker's logo would usually be found. Evita's long black curls are held back with combs, and for a moment she reminded me of Mariapi. A groom leans under the horse's neck and whispers a few words, he gestures towards the stables and I know that my time as a fly on the wall has ended.

Evita walked quickly to the stables, I step forwards- my beautiful dream ended.

"It's good to see you!" She speaks in perfect English, not a trace of a Spanish accent.

"Who taught you the English?"

"Mother taught me," she said proudly and I saw she still wore the locket, the same locket as on her wedding day. With the emblem of the crown of Sevilla inscribed upon it.

"You had the best teacher then..."

"I know," she said, and we walked towards the stables.

Sunlight threw patterns of light and shadow onto the cobbled surface of the yard... it reminded me of her wedding night... the cooking fires and glowing lanterns, the motionless shadow of a dancer on sandy earth...

"Come with me - I show you the boys..."

She paused outside the first loosebox, "This stallion is a distant relative to Ganador and he's from Nevada blood lines."

"What's his name?"

"He's called Reinoso. Look how kingly he stands." In the silvery light he looked unreal, a glossy silver grey coat with black points and dark mane, a longer head with convex nose, which ended in a dark mouth. His aura of dignity was overpowering... but he lacked the special quality that had been Ganador's. He stood watching, majestic and aloof.

"Can you see any resemblance?"

"I don't really know..."

We walked to the next loosebox, where the magnificent bay was stabled- Evita's mount. He stood proudly on a thick bed of golden colored wheat straw. I immediately noticed his strong sinewy joints and hard firm hooves, the arrogant turn of the head, his proud unmoving eyes. "Arrogante," she said "the name seems to suit him..."

She pointed to a third stallion, "The new boy on the block," she said. He was taller and more powerfully built with high striking withers. He had a lovely head and neck, and broad muscular shoulders.

"His nose is somewhat depressed above the nostrils..."

"An oriental characteristic," she said. "He is Hispano Arab. The Andalucian and horses like Grazioso have served Spain well, in war and peace"

"Are there many difficulties when crossing Spanish mares with Arab stallions?"

"The crossing of Spanish with Arab produces a very good first cross, a fair second and then a poor third!"

"I wonder why?"

"No idea"

Just then I heard Marks voice "It must be the weakening of the Spanish line … can't be anything else. We still have a few good Andalucian mares left, not many though. Nothing lasts forever, breeds change and wants differ." He stroked the stallions silky nose "He'd suit you Norma, he's strong and has perfect manners, what you call a gentleman - ideal horse for a lady." His aloof face and broad brow expressed a more nervous delicacy, but still there was something missing. We turned into a further passageway where more stallions were housed. I saw quality Arabian and sleek thoroughbreds, some with racing pedigrees.

Evita opened a window at the bottom of the passageway … "Listen Norma," she said. I looked down over the lovely meadows set around the eucalyptus trees. "It's the end of the day and time for the herdsman to call the mares and foals in from grass." The horses gathered by the gates waiting for his call. Only a few foals had to be called twice, every single one knew their names. The youngsters were full of character. The mares all had wise expressions and dark tranquil eyes. As each family of horses galloped past the sound was of thunder, followed by a drumming rhythm on the hard earth. Thick clouds of dust blocked the light.

"Well … Have you seen a horse you like?"

"I'm not sure-"

"What is it Norma?" Evita could sense my unease

"I think I may have made a mistake."

"Why?"

"In searching for another Ganador …"

For a time, I looked out over the lower meadows, where Ganador had spent his first six months of life with Ganadora. I gazed over the Campina de Sevilla, the pueblo on the hill and the pretty orange plantations … I watched the herdsman finishing his work on the paddocks. Low shafts of sunlight lay across the yard of La Cuadra, like a silver haze, I had made my decision, I would look elsewhere.

22 Campanero Veinte

Estepona Andalucia.

One glorious spring morning, when the grass was green and the fields were rich in a tapestry of poppies and wild orchids, I started my search for a horse. If possible, I would look for the old Baroque type, I knew he must still exist somewhere, and where better to look than Andalucia – this magical corner of Western Europe. I drove towards the lush meadows which surround Estepona, following tracks through hill country then down by rivers. By chance, I passed a stable yard with a small Yeguada sign; it was almost hidden behind towering Eucalyptus trees. Here I was to meet Francisco, a famous rider and authority on the Spanish horse, maybe my lucky star led me to his door.

"Buenos Dias Señora," he said smiling happily before jumping off his horse. "Francisco Tineo," he said bowing, speaking always in his native tongue.

Francisco patiently guided me from beginning to end of his stables, past lines of stalls through into hay barns which led to other smaller adjoining yards. His enthusiasm for the Spanish horse was infectious, his knowledge endless.

But something drew me over to a line of loose boxes Francisco had not shown me. There were four loose boxes almost hidden by trees, all the boxes stood in shade but for one which appeared almost black, the only one with no signs of life.

"New arrivals Señora, the shade is calming," he said in a soft voice.

Inside the darkest loose box standing as far away from the door as possible I glimpsed the outline of a caballo. I felt his breath, sensed his nervous tension, and then I saw his flashing eyes. His eyes followed my every movement and when I spoke he answered in a low melodious whinny.

"Can I see him?" I asked cautiously. Francisco stared at me in surprise before replying.

"Not many people want the old blood lines Señora," he answered patiently. "His breeding is Cartuhano, a little too temperamental for a lady." I knew Francisco was suggesting he had more suitable horses. "Today's buyers want horses with sensible temperaments and three good paces not high stepping chariot horses!" But I persisted and Francisco led him out of the dark box and into the yard.

He was incredibly beautiful; with eyes that seemed to stare directly into mine.

"He's beautiful..." I heard myself say, already in love with this strange stallion.

"He is a pretty one," he conceded. "I was thinking of breaking him to drive."

"Can I see him moving?" I asked, afraid that Francisco would dismiss the idea.

"I can lunge him on the left rein" he said as he walked the stallion onto a sanded area.

"But not to the right?" I asked.

"I will try Señora," he looked at me thoughtfully. "But he may refuse. He's not the type to do anything he doesn't understand." Francisco's doubtful expression told me everything I wanted to know...

Francisco led the stallion to the right before carefully playing the lead out. For a few minutes all was calm then suddenly the stallion froze; head high in the air, hind legs placed well under his body, every joint flexed and prepared for what was to come. With his body coiled together like a spring he jumped into the air travelling forwards for at least ten meters before lightly touching the earth once more.

"Strange horses they are Señora," he said thoughtfully. "No

earthly bred creature would jump like that!" Francisco began to whistle to the stallion, a strange bird like whistle, a sound that calmed him immediately. And I thought of Fernando's words:

'The left and right reins are as unconnected worlds to the Iberian horse, whatever is taught on the left must be taught from the beginning on the right. You must remember his origins, for thousands of years he was ridden by warriors with the reins in the left hand, the spear in the right.'

At that moment I heard the unmistakable noise of Geoff's old truck rattling down the unmade road, before coming to a screaming stop beneath the trees. After a while he found the shady yard beside the lemon grove, where I stood with Francisco.

"Knew I'd find you!" he said, not looking at the object of my desire. "Francisco's son has just shown me his new truck," he said grinning from ear to ear thinking about the miracle on four wheels standing in the yard next to the casa.

"What have you seen?" he asked, after the formalities of meeting Francisco Senior.

"Come and take a look at this boy," I replied "I think I like him." Geoff stared at the young stallion for what felt to be a long minute and then he smiled; a smile of pure happiness.

"So he's coming home to join us ... What is he called?"

"He's called Campanero..."

Much to Francisco's dismay I insisted on purchasing the stallion. What else could I do? No one would ever understand the ways of a creature that could almost fly ... His name is Campanero Veinte, his color is of shining silver and his mane is soft like the finest silk. I fell in love with his flashing black eyes and spirit of fire. He is a little smaller than Ganador, but very noble and stunningly handsome. . . .

Well, I have come to the end of a long road. The Story of Ganador has finally reached its end, as all stories must. I have no sorrow, not now, for I have returned to the land of Ganador's birth, the enchanting Andalucia. It's a place where I can turn my back on what is past and look towards the morning sun. From the terrace of my finca I watch my creature from ancient times cavorting in the same kingly manner as Ganador once did. And as the sun sets behind the tall trees I hear his magical whinnies, so melodious and beautiful.

He is part of history, no more, no less. We are all part of history, living in a time vacuum we call 'the present.' Ganador allowed me to glimpse the past, and in a way I feel thousands of years old. I have peeped into the world of ancient Greece and Rome when men were bold and brave, when the most important thing in life was to ride a noble battle horse.

I have learned there is only one road, the road of truth and learning. It's a road we can travel together. This is our duty; we owe it to our children. To follow the truth and constantly learn from they who are Masters. At last I know where I'm going, the light has been rekindled and is willing to shine once more. Perhaps not as brightly as it shone before, but I will be content with a little...

'He is no normal horse. He is unique in stance, countenance, movement and reaction.
To all who see him he will bring alive the richness of ancient myth and of history.
This horse was bred to be a King
We, his unworthy subjects'

N. Jimenez

End of volume Three.

Brief Index of Equestrian Terms.

Spanish Horse .... Andalucian, Carthusian (Cartuhano) P.R.E. (Pure Raza Espanol)

Lusitano ... Bred in Portugal. The Lusitano is now classed as a separate breed within Portugal.

Stud Farm.

Coudelaria ... Horse breeding ranch - Portugal.

Yeguada ... Horse breeding ranch - Spain.

Airs of the ground.

Piaffe ... Piaffer. A rhythmical trot on the spot appearing to mark time. In the ideal Piaffe the forearm should be raised almost horizontal to the ground.

Passage ... A highly collected trot that appears to hover. The forearm should appear horizontal to the ground and the hind legs step forwards under the body. In the soft passage the rider aims to capture the slow rhythm of passage but not the height.

Pirouette ... Performed in canter or walk. The hindquarters mark the center of the circle, whilst the forelegs mark the circumference. The forelegs move around the hind legs and should cross.

Spanish Walk (Pas d'Espagne) ... The horses forelegs are raised and extended forwards in each step of walk. Its knees should remain straight and the whole movement should appear graceful.

Spanish Trot (Trot d'Espagne) ... The forelegs are raised and extended forwards, as in Spanish walk whilst the hind describe energetic passage like steps. Demands power, ability and perfect balance.

Canter in Place (Ancient Canter)... The horse canters without moving forwards. Canter in place was first trained as a battle movement and used in the gineta skirmish, dual on horseback.

Canter to the rear ... The horse canters in place and shows some movement backwards. This movement is rarely seen. Canter to the rear was needed by warriors in hand to hand mounted combat.

Levade ... Prepared by steps in piaffe, the horse raises his forehand high with hind legs placed neatly under his body which show flexion in all three joints. The Levade began in combat, with less emphasis on correct flexion of hind legs and is still seen in gineta style riding.

Airs above the ground. (Leaps and jumps)

Capriole ... The horse jumps high into the air. At the moment his body is horizontal to the ground he kicks out with both hind legs. It is believed this jump with its deadly kick back was used in battle to injure foot soldiers.

Courbette ... A series of short jumps, off the hind legs without the forelegs touching the ground. The movement is performed from a levade or rear.

High school airs are divided into two categories: Airs from the ground and Airs above the ground. These airs demand great ability, strength and perfect athleticism.